THE MESSENGER

Center Point
Large Print

Also by Bill Brooks and available from
Center Point Large Print:

The Journey of Jim Glass series
  A Bullet for Billy
  The Horses

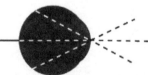

**This Large Print Book carries the
Seal of Approval of N.A.V.H.**

THE MESSENGER

A Western Story

BILL BROOKS

CENTER POINT LARGE PRINT
THORNDIKE, MAINE

This Center Point Large Print edition is published
in the year 2013 in conjunction with
Golden West Literary Agency.

The text of this Large Print edition is unabridged.
In other aspects, this book may vary
from the original edition.
Printed in the United States of America
on permanent paper.
Set in 16-point Times New Roman type.

ISBN: 978-1-61173-780-6

Library of Congress Cataloging-in-Publication Data

Brooks, Bill, 1943–
The messenger / Bill Brooks.
pages ; cm.
ISBN 978-1-61173-780-6 (library binding : alk. paper)
1. Life change events—Fiction. 2. Large type books. I. Title.
PS3552.R65863M47 2013
813'.54—dc22
                                                        2012051790

For Bob and his beautiful daughters,
Maggie and Claire

Part of the cursedness of the shotgun messenger's life—the loneliness of it. He is like a sheep dog, feared by the flock and hated by the wolves. On the stage he is a necessary evil. Passengers and driver alike regard him with aversion, without him and his pestilential box their lives would be ninety percent safer and they know it. The bad men, the rustlers—the stage robbers actual and potential—hate him. They hate him because he is the guardian of property, because he stands between them and their desires, because they will have to kill him before they can get their hands into the coveted box. Most of all they hate him because of his shotgun—the homely weapon that makes him the peer of many armed men in a quick turmoil of powder and lead.

Wyatt Earp

Chapter One

The day had started off fine enough. The air was clean and crisp and the mountains shone in the distance and the river ran clear and bright.

Ophelia and I had made love just before dawn broke. An hour later we all sat at the table eating a breakfast of flapjacks covered in molasses, fried ham, and coffee.

My boy, Nicholas, just turned ten the week before, sat across from me, a reflection of myself at that age. A hank of wheat-colored hair fell unruly over his forehead. He ate like he had to catch a train and was already late.

We were a happy little family. After years of me being a loose-footed rambler, I'd finally found what I'd been looking for—love and peace.

Nobody could know that tragedy was less than an hour away.

I was in the garden, hoeing weeds out between the rows of chest-high corn when it happened.

I heard Ophelia scream, looked up, then toward where she pointed, toward the river that came down from somewhere high up in the mountains, down through a stand of loblolly pine and snaked below our cabin.

Nicholas was drawn to the river every free

minute he wasn't doing chores or his studies, which Ophelia was strict about.

"Don't want you growing up ignorant as a stick," she'd tell him whenever he bucked against the traces of responsibility. "You want to end up swamping out saloons?"

He'd grin that winning smile at her and try to win her over to his side of things—why it was more important to catch fish or go hunting with me than it was to learn multiplication tables—but she stood firm on his learning.

But it was Sunday and she let him enjoy himself, saying even God took his leisure on Sunday.

The reason for her startled scream was a dark shape moving with unbelievable speed toward Nicholas who stood frozen, watching the thing, too. A big grizzly. It had come from the dark stand of pines upstream. It must have seen my son and saw him as an easy kill.

I ran without thinking, the hoe still in my hand. There wasn't any time to go to the house and get my gun.

The distance was two hundred yards easily from garden to river, but on a downward slope. I yelled all the way, screaming for Nicholas to lay down, curl up. Running would only incite the bear. I knew this from an old man who used to do nothing but hunt them. He said the worst thing you could do was look a bear in the eyes or run from one.

"Ain't no human alive can outrun a bear. They can be fast as a race horse in a short distance."

This one was, a rippling mass of dark fur and muscle. Its neck and head were extended, its big paws tossing up loose clods of earth.

"Get down, Nick! Get down!"

But my son did what just about anybody would do. He ran.

I had halved the distance between us when the bear took him down. Ophelia had stopped screaming. I don't know why other than she was probably just frozen with fear.

I couldn't see my son under the bear. It was hunched over him, tearing at him. It felt like my feet didn't even touch the ground.

I could hear its huffs and I swung the hoe blade as hard as I could and struck it across the neck, and it jumped and turned on me. I swung again and nearly cut off its nose, and it roared and fell back away, hurt, because the old bear hunter had said to me: "You ever find yourself in a tangle with a bear and you got no gun or knife, jab its eyes or hit it in the nose . . . that's your best chance if you got any at all."

The piece of nose dangled from the end of its brutal face, and it turned and ran off back toward the woods, and I picked up my son.

His head was bloody and he was limp, not moving or even breathing. I didn't want to believe he was all that hurt as I rushed back to the house,

11

meeting Ophelia halfway up the hill, her face stark and drained of color, her mouth open in a wordless cry.

A bear knows how to kill quick, like any predator.

I laid Nicholas out on the kitchen table so we could wash the blood off him and see how bad he was hurt. But I already knew he was dead. I just didn't want to believe it.

Ophelia worked feverishly over him, speaking his name in a pleading way.

Finally I put my arms around her to stop her.

"He's gone," I said.

"No," she said.

She fought to free herself of me, turned her anger and fear and pain on me, and I didn't try and stop her from beating at me with her fists. I felt the same fear and anger and pain, but I couldn't do anything about it.

Finally she collapsed in my arms and I held her for the longest time—until she stopped sobbing. Then she seemed to gather herself and said softly: "I have to wash his little body and dress him in a clean set of clothes. You dig him a grave."

It almost sounded like someone else speaking from within her, a stranger who'd come to the house to take care of matters.

I went out and began digging the grave, west of the house with a fine view of the river.

I dug until my hands were blistered and

bleeding, until my eyes filled and stung with tears, until curses escaped my breath.

I blamed myself for not saving my son, for moving here to this wilderness instead of in a town somewhere. I had to have openness, be surrounded by trees and mountains and a river. I'd bought the place with the cabin on it from the old bear hunter who'd told me about how bears acted. He claimed he'd killed them all out and was moving on farther up into the mountains.

"Where there is still some bar," he had said. "I can't stand no kind of civilization and I can't stand no place where there ain't bar."

That was five years earlier.

The bears had come back. At least one had.

We wrapped our son in a handmade quilt given us on our wedding day by Ophelia's folks along with $200, "to fix up that old Stevens place," her pa said. They were both good people.

If there had been time and I had the right tools I would have built my son a coffin, but I had neither. I had grief and vengeance on my mind even as I laid to rest our only child, even as I shoveled in the dirt over him and carried large stones to stack on his grave so no animal could dig it up.

Ophelia stood silent the whole time. I think she'd gone away in her mind and wasn't coming back anytime soon.

Some storm clouds grew dark over the

mountains and by nightfall there was a heavy rain drumming down on the roof. Ophelia sat in a rocker staring into the dark shadows where Nicholas's little room stood just off the kitchen.

I knew what I had to do.

In the morning I packed a horse and saddled another.

She stood watching me.

"Don't leave me," she said.

"I got to go," I said.

"For what reason?"

"You already know."

"No. It won't change anything. It's too late, Royce."

"Maybe it is for him," I said, looking off to the pile of stones, the wood cross I'd lashed together. "But I aim to find that god damn' bear and lay waste to it."

"And if you don't come back?"

"Why wouldn't I come back?"

The fear in her eyes was something she couldn't hide.

I slid the brass-fitted Henry into the scabbard.

"No bear will stand up against this," I said.

"I'll hate you if you go and leave me."

"I got no choice. I can't just sit here and do nothing."

She turned her gaze away from me. What was left of her spirit, I thought, had gone where the souls of the forever heartbroken go and don't return. Still, I couldn't get beyond my own mad heart, my own taste and need to avenge my son's death. *Our* son's death.

"I'll kill it and be back in under a week," I said.

She didn't say anything.

I rode away feeling I'd lost everything. I was right. I had.

Chapter Two

Summer turned to autumn and autumn turned to winter and the snow trapped me up in those high mountains. By then I'd killed twenty-three bears and not one of them with a cut nose.

I aimed to quit, to go home, but then the snow came heavily one night and I woke up under it and I was sure by the end of that day I was going to die in those mountains along with the bears I'd killed, that it was some sort of strange way God had of testing me. Like I was Job or somebody.

But I'd stopped believing in any sort of God the day my son was killed and I cursed Him even though I did not believe. I cursed Him every day up in those mountains and I cursed Him for wanting to kill me by freezing me to death.

As luck would have it, I found the old bear hunter—his shack, at least, and what was left of him. He was sitting upright in a snowdrift, frozen white, one hand reaching for the sky, his eyes wide and staring and glazed over, his mouth open.

I couldn't do anything for him as nearly frozen as I was.

The shack was the size of a single room but it had a wood burner in it—the one I'd seen him pack on the back of his mule that day he had sold me the cabin and went off. And there was some split wood to feed it and a nice narrow hand-hewn bed with a rope mattress and blankets.

A necklace of bear claws lay on a small table along with a few cans of beans and peaches.

The wind blew hard for five straight days and the snow piled up to the roof. When it quit, the old man was buried somewhere under it, and I thought it was just as well since I had no tools for digging a grave even if there was a way to dig one in that frozen ground.

I ached to get back home again, but there wasn't any way—not till spring. I cursed every-thing and everyone I could think of, then I lost my mind for a while.

By spring I couldn't even find a shoe from the old man. Something had come and dragged him off, had clawed through the snow to get him. I figured it couldn't be a bear since they denned in the winter. But something had got him.

Only one of my horses survived. I ate most of the other one.

Then I made my way back home again.

Ophelia and some of her things were gone.

A note lay on the kitchen table where we last ate a happy breakfast with our son.

Dere Royce,
   Just as you've left me, I've left you. Please don't come in search of me. Things can't ever be the same between us. I hope you didn't die up in the mountains looking for your dam bear. I hope you find a new life. Just as I seek to find my own.

Ophelia

I read it a dozen times hoping the words would change. But they never did. I found an old bottle of bourbon left over from a long time ago and drank it straight until it was empty, and I fell drunk out on the porch and lay there a long time with the world around me spinning. I knew liquor could cause some men to forget their troubles, or at least make them seem not so bad. It didn't mine.

But I passed out from the long journey, weariness, frustration at never finding *my* bear, and now my wife had gone off.

I thought about putting my pistol to my head and ending it. What did I have to live for?

But in the end it seemed to me the coward's way out and I knew I was a lot of things, but I wasn't any coward.

I saddled my horse, rolled up what few belongings I had into my sougan—a couple of shirts, extra pair of denim trousers, socks, soap and razor, and a tintype of the three of us taken in a photographer's studio in Bozeman the year before the bear came out of the woods. I lashed it to the back of my saddle, filled my saddle pockets with extra shells, some beef jerky I found in one of the jars, and slid the Henry into the scabbard.

I burned the house and rode away in search of Ophelia.

Chapter Three

The summer and fall came and went before I found her.

I was in a saloon in Butte when I heard about a woman they called the Rose of Cimarron, a prostitute they said was the best-looking whore any of them had ever seen. I heard one patron describe her as having a rose-shaped stain on her hip and that's how she come by the name.

Ophelia had a rose-shaped stain on her right hip, a birthmark.

It was hard news to hear and I wanted to kill the fellow who said it. But he was just talking about a woman he didn't know and couldn't understand and I was relieved to have found her.

I asked him about the Rose of Cimarron and how I could find her. He told me and I went to the place and stood there at the foot of the outdoor stairs, looking up at the lighted window. It was near Christmas and cold with patches of old snow on the ground that looked ghostly. I heard the laughter of men up in that room and saw shadows pass back and forth behind the yellow light of the window.

I drew my piece and held it in my hand when the door opened and two cowboys stepped out onto the landing, still laughing over something.

I waited till they descended the stairs, then stepped out of the shadows, my piece cocked and aimed.

They stopped dead in their tracks, their hands instinctively raising, open so I could see they had nothing in them.

"What you want, mister?" one of them said. He was tall and lanky, wearing a sheepskin coat. His hat was high-crowned with a feather in the band. He looked like a kid. The other one was older, shorter by a head. He had long dark moustaches and a crooked nose.

"I aim to kill you," I said.

"For what reason?" the older one said.

"Just for being in the wrong place," I said.

They looked at each other disbelieving that such a good time had suddenly turned into a bad one.

"Are you crazy?"

"No," I said.

Then suddenly something unexpected happened. The shorter man pulled his piece fast as any draw I'd ever seen, just as the taller one crossed in front of him.

The gunshot echoed in the dark cold night like somebody had just slammed shut a door. The taller one staggered from the punch of the bullet in his back, then fell into a pile of dirty snow, screaming.

"You shot me, Daddy!" he yelped.

The shooter stood, disbelieving. He looked at me.

"Put your damn' gun down," I said. "Help your kid to his feet and get the hell out of here."

He did as ordered, the kid still yelping, blood dripping from somewhere under his coat, but he did not look near fatally wounded.

They staggered off into the shadows and out toward the street.

I climbed the stairs and knocked on the door.

She opened it.

We stood there, looking at each other. She was worn and thin and looked as if she'd aged twenty years. Her hair was tangled about her head and her eyes were red and cheeks sallow. She was skin and bone, standing there nearly naked in a cotton shift.

At first she didn't recognize me. I'd let my beard grow all that previous year until now. I kept meaning to shave it off but hadn't. I must have looked like hell, too.

"Ophelia," I said.

Then her eyes widened.

"What are you doing here?" she said.

"I come to get you."

"Get me for what?"

"Take you home." Then I remembered we had no home. I'd burned it to the ground. But I'd get another home and we'd start over and we'd have another son and things would go back to how they were even though the grief for Nicholas was still in my heart like a dagger.

"Take me home?" she said.

"Yes."

"This is my home."

I pushed past her and closed the door behind me.

It was what they called a crib—the lowest form of prostitutes were the crib girls—a small spare room with only a bed and a chamber pot, a tin pitcher and pan with water and a rag floating in it on a little stand by the bed. Next to the pan was a bottle half full of liquor.

"Get the hell out of here!" she said. "Or I'll call the law."

I took off my hat and combed back my hair with my fingers.

"I made a mistake by leaving you once," I said. "I'm not going to leave you again. Put your things together and let's go."

"You go . . . straight to hell, Royce Blood."

It tore me up inside to hear her talk that way. But I was determined. I was taking her with me.

She turned and grabbed the liquor bottle and tipped it to her mouth and drank.

"You want anything else it will cost you three dollars," she said.

I just stood there, trying to find the right words.

"You shoot those damn' cowboys?" she said. "I heard a gunshot."

"No, I didn't shoot anybody."

She laughed in the false way people do when they want to mock you.

"Those boys will go get their friends and come back and drag you with a rope until you're just rags," she said. "You better get the hell out before they do."

"I told you, I'm not leaving here without you," I said.

"Then you'll be waiting a damn' long time."

I grabbed the bottle from her hand and she slapped me.

I saw the look in her eyes as soon as she did. She started to cry.

"Let it be," I said. "Just let all of it be and come home with me."

"No," she said. "I can't go back there."

"Then we'll go somewhere else."

"No."

"I shouldn't have left you, Ophelia. I know that now. I was just all screwed up in my head. Can't a man make a mistake and own up to it?"

"You left me," she said again. "When I needed you the most, you just left me."

"I know it," I said, my own words breaking apart as they came out.

She started to cough and the coughs racked her entire thin body. She spat into the pan, and it was a bloody foam. I took hold of her as she started to shiver, grabbed the spread off the bed, and wrapped it around her.

"I'm freezing," she whispered. "I can't stop shaking."

And yet her skin was fevered, so warm I could feel her heat through my own clothes.

I lay on the bed with her, holding her close.

She coughed and shook, and I held her until she settled some. The minutes and hours crawled, but soon enough she fell asleep, and still I held her and somewhere in the long night I feel asleep, too, and dreamed.

The dream was of the three of us, picnicking under a large tree, the grass all around us tall and leaning over in the wind, the sky above blue and full of large fluffy clouds, Nicholas saying they were sailing ships in the sky. Then something dark loomed over us. The bear. I shot it, one, two, three times. The bang of my pistol was sharp and loud.

Only it wasn't my pistol but someone banging on the door. I started, reaching for my gun.

"Alice!" a voice yelled. "Alice, you in there? Open up!"

I went to the door, gun in hand, cocked and aimed and ready, and opened it.

A large man with heavy red moustaches stood on the landing. His hat had snowflakes on it that were falling out of a red sky and into the light cast from inside the room.

He looked at the piece in my hand, then past me trying to see into the room. Behind him lined up on the stairs were three other men in heavy coats. One of them had a scarf tied round the crown of his hat and under his chin.

"Alice?" the man on the landing said again.

"She's asleep," I said.

He looked at me with his heavy lidded eyes. His jowls hung like slabs of ham.

"You might want to put that hog-leg down," he said. "Before it goes off accidental."

"It won't go off accidental," I said. "It goes off, it will be on purpose."

"I'm here to arrest you," he said. "Sheriff John Poe is my name." He turned his head slightly. "These are my deputies."

"Arrest me for what?"

"Shooting Willy Nickel," he said.

"I didn't shoot anybody. It was his old man who shot him."

He shifted his gaze to back over my shoulder again, then to my piece.

"I guess we'll figure it all out once we see the judge," he said. "What'd you do with Alice?"

"Her name's not Alice," I said. "I'm her husband. Now leave us the hell alone."

He blinked. Snow still fell on his hat.

"Husband? I didn't know she was married."

"She is."

"I want to have a look-see, make sure she's all right."

"She's sick with fever."

"We need to work this out," he said.

"Nothing to work out," I said.

"Them fellows are off the Double Bar," he said. "They'll go back and round up their *compadres* and come back and tear this town up looking to kill you."

"Then there will be some blood shed," I said.

He shook his head. "How about I get a doc for Alice, and then you come by my office first thing, and we'll talk about your future?"

"OK," I said.

I closed the door and heard them clomping back down the stairs. I had noticed the silver wedding band the sheriff was wearing, figured he was a practical man when it came to dying, figured that's why he was willing to back off. Me, I had nothing to lose.

I turned back to the bed where Ophelia lay.

I knew soon as I touched her that she was dead.

Somewhere in the long night of our sorrow, she had passed. I wanted to believe her spirit was with that of Nicholas's, that they were walking

together on streets of gold. But I'd lost whatever faith I'd had in such things up in those
mountains, ruminating on why my boy had been
killed by the bear.

I poured fresh water into the pan after throwing
out the old and washed her body, taking tender
care. Her legs and arms were scabbed over in
places from old sores. Her ribs ridged under her
skin. Her mouth was still delicate but that was all.
I brushed her hair, found a fresh nightgown in
the little trunk—one I remembered seeing her in
during the happier days of our lives. It was
trimmed in silk ribbons. And when I finished, it
looked like she was just sleeping.

I lay back down beside her and held her for the
last time in my arms and slept peaceful for an
hour or two. Whenever it was, the first cold gray
light of dawn came in through the window like
some old cat creeping into the room and crawled
up on the bed and lay softly over us.

I rose and put on my hat and coat and stepped
outside into the brittle air and drew it deeply
into my lungs, then descended the stairs.

I walked into town and met a man sweeping
out front of his storefront and asked him if there
was a mortician. He directed me to the barbershop, and I went up there and waited until a
fellow in a derby hat arrived, high-stepping across
the muddy street, the patches of snow, and
puddles of dirty water.

"You need a haircut or a burying?" he said.

"Burying," I said.

"Obviously not you," he said.

"Obviously not," I said.

We went inside and the room smelled of toilet water and soap, and there was a barber's chair with a padded leather seat and a shelf of bottles and a mirror.

"My funeral business is in the back," he said, indicating a room behind a curtain.

I told him about Ophelia—the woman they called the Rose of Cimarron, or Alice—and he nodded.

"Didn't know she was a married woman," he said, hanging up his coat and hat. He was bald. I thought barbering an odd profession for somebody without any hair.

I explained what I wanted.

He gave me a price.

"I want a priest for her, too."

"Not a problem," he said.

I wondered privately if he had been with her at one time or another. Then I pushed away the thought. I paid him.

"See it gets done today," I said.

"Yes, sir."

I asked him how to get to the sheriff's office, and he told me.

I went up there.

The old man was sitting behind his desk,

drinking coffee when I entered. He looked half surprised to see me.

"How's Alice . . . I mean your wife doing?" he said.

"She died."

His brows furrowed.

"Sorry to hear."

"What'd you want to see me about?" I said. "You still planning on arresting me? Because I'm not going to let you arrest me."

I could see that didn't please him much. I didn't care if it pleased him or not.

"Those boys from the Double Bar . . . ," he started to say.

"To hell with them. I'm not running."

"Nobody asked you to run."

"Sounds like that's what you were suggesting."

He shook his head, blew steam from his cup, holding it in both hands. It was a china cup with blue figures painted on it.

"Them boys stick tight together," he said.

"Then they'll die together," I said.

He sipped some of his coffee, looked thoughtful, grandfatherly, for a moment.

"What is it . . . you want to stay around for the funeral, or just raise holy hell in my town, or what?"

"I'm not staying for the funeral," I said.

"I'll see to it the town pays for her expenses."

"Don't bother. They're already paid for."

28

"Then what is it you want?"

"I want to kill somebody," I said.

"Kill somebody? For what reason?"

"I don't know. I just do."

"Son, that's a bad way to think."

"I know it."

"I believe you about the other night, that the kid's old man shot him. I've no intention of arresting you. But I've no intention of letting you stay any longer in my town than necessary, either. You want some coffee?"

"No," I said.

"Sometimes life is just plain shit," he said.

I nodded, walked out and back down the street, mounted my horse, and rode away.

Chapter Four

I began to drink hard. I was looking for trouble, looking for a way to shed myself of my anger and hurt, and there wasn't any better way of doing that than getting drunk and looking for trouble, a fistfight or gunfight. I wanted to hurt somebody and I wanted to hurt them bad. I was hoping maybe somebody would kill me, do the job I couldn't bring myself to do.

I'd get drunk, get into fights, but nobody killed me. I don't know why they didn't. I just didn't run into the right man is all I could figure.

I drifted aimlessly from town to town, letting my horse decide the journey we'd travel. We tended to drift sideways, north and south, east and west. I don't know what that damned horse was thinking except grass, water, rest.

I'd fall off it drunk sometimes, and, whenever I'd wake on the ground, I was surprised it hadn't run off on me or somebody hadn't stolen it.

I'd run out of money drinking, and then find some sort of menial work—just enough to buy me another bottle, maybe a cot for the night in out of the cold and rain and wind. I ate little, lost weight. I saw myself in a storefront window once and didn't recognize myself. My beard had gotten long.

I hocked my guns in Belle Fouche just for some whiskey, a little food. The man gave me $15 for my Henry and my pistol. I kept drifting all that winter and into the summer and on through it into the autumn.

I finally drifted into Deadwood Gulch. I got drunk, fell off my horse. I woke up and saw an old miner's shack with the door missing. I crawled inside and fell upon the cot. The mattress was gone and the windows busted out and the walls were covered in old newspaper and catalogue pages that were curled and yellow and brittle as butterfly wings.

I don't know how long I slept.

I woke to the sound of a hard rain shattering

against the tin roof. I was shivering from the cold. I got up and poked around inside the potbelly stove standing in one corner of the room. There wasn't anything inside but ashes and a rat's skeletal remains.

I cursed my luck. I'd stopped cursing God sometime back. What was the point of cursing something I no longer believed in?

I flopped back down again, covering myself the best I could with my sougan.

Next thing I knew I sold my horse and saddle. I bought more whiskey and carried it back to the shack. I figured maybe I might drink myself into a stupor I'd never wake from. Fine by me if it happened.

Then came a voice from the past, one I never thought I'd hear again.

"Hullo, the house!"

It was impossible to mistake the raspy voice of Burt Bee. After two long hard summers on the Texas plains skinning buffalo, I'd gotten to know the voice well enough.

Burt had suffered some sort of childhood accident. Actually he'd nearly hanged himself trying to swing out of a haymow with a towel tied around his head, playing like he was a pirate, swinging from one ship to another. Only the rope tangled around his neck. And if he hadn't been such a big kid and the rope hadn't been so frayed, he said he would have long been in his grave.

I yelled for him to come on in and he did.

He stood there, dripping rain off his hat brim and slicker.

"How'd you know I was here?" I said, sitting up, my head feeling busted.

"I thought I recognized you when you come into Mann's Number Ten saloon the other day. I couldn't be sure it was you because of all that hair you growed on your face, so I thought I'd stop 'round and see."

"Well, now you've seen," I said.

"So I have. I figured to see Jesus before I seen you again," he said.

"Maybe I'm Him," I said.

He cracked a smile, showing he still had most of his teeth.

"Well, if you are Him, then all is lost and a lot of them churchgoers will probably be committing suicide."

Burt always was a funny son-of-a-bitch.

"What you doing in the gulch?" he said.

"I don't know. Trying to die, I reckon."

"You look pretty close to it already."

I looked down at my dirty union suit.

"I reckon so."

"Last I heard of you, you was married with some kids living up in Wyoming Territory," he said.

"Montana," I corrected.

"Hell, it's all pretty much the same country, ain't it."

"Yeah, I suppose you could look at it that way. What about you?"

"Me?" He grinned again. "I'm driving stage in this bunghole."

"That sounds like a promotion from what you were doing back last time I saw you."

He looked around.

"Clem Small leave you this place?"

"Who's Clem Small?" I said.

"Was a miner."

"He must have, because he sure as hell wasn't here when I got here, and you know what they say about finders keepers."

"You look like you could stand a good meal," he said.

"I could stand a lot of things, but a meal is least on my list."

"What's first?"

"A drink."

He shook his head, took off his hat and shook it, then set it back on his head again. He took up nearly the entire room. I never had to worry about getting jumped back in those wild Texas towns when we were skinners because just to look at him would put doubt in your mind no matter how mean and drunk and looking for a fight you might be. I'd seen him whip four men one night in a bagnio in Mobeetie—one of them nearly to death. Burt had a bloody nose was all.

"Tell you what, I'll buy you a drink after I buy you a meal, how will that be?"

"That'd be fine."

"Get some clothes on . . . we may be wild and woolly and hell on wheels around here, but at least we go out of doors fully dressed."

"You sure ask a lot of a fellow," I said.

"You smell like you could use a bath too."

"Well, let's not go overboard," I said.

"Hell," he said, and waited outside for me.

Chapter Five

Deadwood Gulch was mostly just a slash between the Black Hills, like somebody had cut a road through it to find whatever gold they were looking for.

The Sioux didn't take kindly to white men coming without being invited, and, from what little I'd read and heard before arriving there— back in my sober days—they were still finding white bodies in the hills around the gulch stuck so full of arrows they looked like big porcupines.

The government sent Custer up there to clean out the Indians, and instead they cleaned him out. It proved to be the last big fight the Indians were ever going to win. The United States Army came in full force and chased most of them all the way to Canada. But I bet they were still smiling about whipping Custer's bony ass.

I followed Burt to a little restaurant jammed cheek to jowl between a saddlery and a dentist office. We took seats by the fly-specked window.

"Doc Holliday used to practice his trade next door," Burt said, settling his hat on a knob of his chair. "I met him once. Eyes like a dead fish, that one."

We ordered the stew and biscuits, coffee, and for dessert vinegar pie. I was surprised how hungry I was, then had to excuse myself out the back door so I could puke it all up. My stomach didn't know much about real food or lots of it; it had grown more accustomed to liquor.

I came back in and sat down again as if nothing was wrong. Burt had ordered a second plate and was halfway through it. He looked up at me with those horse-big eyes of his.

"You OK?"

"Never been better," I said.

He went back to eating like he was alone. I sat there and sipped the rest of the coffee in my cup.

Burt paid the bill and left a 10¢ tip. Then we walked over to Mann's Number Ten and took up residence, and Burt had a bottle and two glasses brought to our table. I pointed to a chair hung up high on the wall and said: "What the hell they got that chair up there for?"

He glanced at it.

"That's the chair Wild Bill was sitting in when McCall shot out his lights." Then he pointed to a stain on the floorboards. "And that is where old Bill fell dead, bleeding out."

"Well, it does bring a certain comfort," I said. "Knowing this is such a safe place to drink."

Burt cracked another grin.

"So you was married, or did I hear that wrong?"

"You heard right."

"Where she at now?"

"Butte, Montana Territory," I said.

"Divorce you?"

"Death divorced us."

He sort of nodded. "Sorry to hear."

"Not as sorry as me."

"Kids?"

"Had one. He's dead, too."

"Again, sorry to hear. You'll have to forgive my ignorance, prying into your affairs."

"You're forgiven."

He poured me a drink, noting I guess how much my hands shook.

"Here's too olden times, back before life became brutal."

"It always was, don't you think?"

"We had us some good times. You remember Bigfoot Simmons?"

Bigfoot was an ace shooter and probably killed more damned buffalo than any man alive. I never saw anyone with his eye or ability in long shooting.

36

"Sure," I said.

"Well, he ended up taking his own life in a hotel in Cleveland, Ohio. Shot himself in the brains. I guess when the buff ran out and he didn't have nothing else to shoot, he just shot himself out of sheer boredom. I think about him sometimes and wonder if maybe we won't all end up that way, civilized as everything's becoming."

"You think?"

"I do," he said, and we swallowed down our whiskey.

Burt refilled our glasses. "Every day we live, we just got those memories of how it was even as we're watching how it's getting to be. Why, do you know, they already got telephones in some of the hotels in Cheyenne?"

I said I did not know that.

He shook his head. "I hate to think what this country will be like twenty years from now."

"You think either of us will live that long?" I said.

He looked at me down the length of his long nose. "I plan on it, but you might be a little less likely, looking at you now."

"You ever had it real good once, you'll know why I'm the way I am now."

"Love of a woman . . . ," he said without finishing the thought.

He poured us another. My hands were starting to shake less.

We talked about the old days there in the Texas Panhandle before he went his way and I went mine.

"You remember that gal, Juanita?" he said.

"The fat one?"

"No, the skinny one with the crossed eyes."

"I remember one of them was crossed."

"That's the one."

"What about her?" I said.

"Nothing. She just come to mind is all."

"You were in love with her, weren't you?"

"Hell, I thought I was till I caught her going at it with Bigfoot in his wagon." He looked suddenly forlorn, then brightened again quick as a storm cloud passing through an otherwise sun-filled sky. "You know what we ought to do?"

"What?"

"Go get us each a bath over in Chiney town, let them Chiney gals wash us."

"I'd just as soon sit here and drink your whiskey," I said.

"We'll get another bottle and take it with us," he said.

"Lead the way," I said.

And so we went to Chiney town and let the Chiney gals wash our hair and everything else as well.

Chapter Six

The next couple of days were a fog of liquor and sex. The Chiney gal in the tub with me was the first woman I'd had who wasn't my wife in fifteen years. Her skin was smooth, the color of almonds, her hair like black silk. She was small and pretty, and, if I'd been sober and of a different frame of mind altogether, I might even have fallen in love with her.

But my heart still belonged to Ophelia and probably always would, and I chalked up my unfaithfulness to the liquor. When I came fully sober again, I came to in my shack, alone and feeling empty. Money only buys you company for so long, even if it is somebody else's money, and my Chiney gal was probably washing another man's hair about now, and I wasn't even a recent memory to her.

I felt as dry and wasted as the deserts down in Mexico.

As if summoned, Burt returned, only this time it was snow he shook off his hat as he stood in the room, and it was snow that melted off his boots, leaving little dark puddles on the floorboards.

"I see you survived," he said.

"I see you did, too."

He had the look of the cat that ate the canary.

"Take more than a couple of Chiney gals to do me in," he said.

"You don't have a whiskey on you, do you?" I said.

"I ain't no sot."

"I reckon I am."

"I reckon," he said.

"What you doing here?" I said.

"Come to see if you wanted some work."

"I think I'm all set," I said.

He looked around at my impoverishment, not even so much as a single can of beans on the shelf above the single-plate potbelly stove. "Well, I can sure see you're living high and mighty and a fellow of your means would see honest work as beneath him and all."

"What sort of work?" I said.

"Riding messenger on my run to Cheyenne."

"Messenger?"

"You still know how to shoot, don't you?"

"Is that what I have to do, shoot somebody?"

"You might."

"I've got no gun."

"I've got a sweet little ten-gauge over at the office you can use. It's got sawn-off barrels and a sawn-off stock and you can hide it under your coat."

"Why would I want to?"

"You wouldn't. I'm just saying if you wanted to. Say if you were going to walk into a bank and rob it, and you didn't want nobody to see you had a shotgun."

"Oh."

"Anyways, my regular messengers . . . both of 'em . . . are unavailable at present. One's down with the gout and the other is being chased by an irate husband and I don't know of anybody I could put stock in except you to see the job through."

"You think you can put stock in me?" I said, doubtful of my own condition.

"I always knew you to be a stick-to-it fellow. I never knew you to quit nothing once you put your hand to it. And I also never knew you to run from a fight if there was one. That's the sort of man I need riding in the box with me."

"Well, hell, you make me sound almost princely," I said.

"You want the job or not?"

"What's the pay?"

"Oh, now you're choosy of a sudden?"

I nodded.

"Fifty dollars. I'll give you half now and half when we get back."

I tried to picture it, me riding hung over atop a stage wagon. It hurt my already hurting head.

"Well?" Burt said, impatient.

"Let me check my schedule," I said.

"Hell," he said, and walked out.

I sat there, thinking about it for a long time. Until I began to shiver again. I pulled on my clothes, boots, coat, and hat, and headed down the road toward town. Maybe if I had something to do, I wouldn't think about having nothing to do. I was flat broke and even a suicidal man gets hungry.

I found Burt in the stage line office. Out front stood a four-horse team of chestnuts hitched into the traces of a Concord, its top painted red and its belly painted yellow.

I stepped inside and Burt looked up from his desk. He was signing papers of some sort. There were five passengers in the office as well. Two of them were a well-dressed couple. The male looked like he had money and the female looked like she did, too. Both handsome and not seeming to fit the usual types Deadwood seemed to attract. Then there was what looked like a rancher with his peaked hat and lace-up boots sitting on a bench along one wall, smoking a cheroot whose smoke wreathed around his head like a small blue cloud. Of the other two fellows, one looked hard and well-used, with a face that looked like it was chiseled from flint. He was wearing a short, blanket coat and I could see the end of a leather holster poking below the hem. The last fellow was a Chinaman dressed like Chinamen dressed in cotton clothes, coat, and a silk cap. He had a rope of black hair hanging partway down his back and he averted his eyes as if he were in the presence of kings.

"I'm glad you were able to clear your schedule," Burt said, and nodded toward the 10-gauge leaning in the corner near his desk. I walked over, hefted it. It felt about right. I cracked it open and saw both chambers were seated with shells.

"You got any more shells for this?" I said.

He looked at the passengers, then at me.

"You planning on starting a war?"

"I'd rather have more and not need them than not to have them and need them," I said.

He pulled a wax box from a drawer and set it atop his desk.

"Take all you want," he said.

I took them all, shook them out, and divided them equally into my coat pockets. They balanced me out the way I thought I should be.

"Let's get them loaded up," Burt said, all officious.

So I went out and held the stage door open, after pulling out the step, and waited for them to load up. All, except for the Chinaman who climbed up on top of the stage, knowing he was probably not welcome among the white passengers inside.

The weather had socked in heavy in the gulch. Thick gray clouds and mist, as though heaven itself had lowered down so common man could reach it because there wasn't any other way most of the inhabitants of Deadwood were ever going to rise up and get to a higher sort of heaven.

Then Burt and me loaded the luggage into the

43

boot along with some mail sacks. Then we went back inside and took a hefty strongbox from inside a safe and carried it out to the stage, and it took all the muscle we had to get it up into the box where Burt locked it into the floor by way of an eye bolt and metal strap with a big brass lock.

He handed me the key and said: "You hold onto this since you're the one with the blaster."

"Thanks," I said. "It means they'll have to kill me to get the key."

He grinned his usual grin, then said: "You coming, or what?"

I climbed up the left-hand side and settled in next to him, my head like a dinner bell being clanged.

"Hold on," he said, and let loose the footbrake, then snapped the reins yelling: "Git up there girls!" Then off we went into the icy fog, and it didn't take but a few minutes to feel like we were lost in a world not of our own making.

I could smell the pitch of pine sweet in the air and wouldn't have been surprised if an arrow came and found one or the other of us.

"Keep a sharp eye," Burt said.

"I don't know how I could see anything in this," I said.

"Keep a sharp eye anyway."

I said I would. The rocking of the stage on its suspension made me queasy even though I hadn't eaten or drunk anything for the last twenty-four hours, although I couldn't remember exactly.

"You look about sick," Burt said, and took a small pint bottle out of his coat pocket and handed it to me. "Try a taste of this."

I read the label.

"This is peach schnapps," I said.

"I know it," he said. "Good for the stomach and the cold."

"It's what women drink," I said.

"Give it back if you don't want any."

I pulled the stopper and took a swallow. It turned warm inside me, like a soft sweet heat flowing down into my belly.

Burt reached for it, and I handed it back. He took a drink, then handed it back and I took another.

"See," he said.

"See what?" I said.

"You feel better already, don't you?"

"I reckon, some."

"See," he said again.

"It ain't so bad if you don't mind drinking like a woman," I said.

"I don't mind," he said, and cracked the bull-whip out over the horses just for the hell of it I think.

It sounded like a pistol shot.

Chapter Seven

We'd changed teams twice and were on our way to Broke Creek station when Burt said: "There's something I ought to tell you about before we get there."

We'd gone almost sixty miles and evening was falling fast because of the time of year it was. The weather had cleared somewhat, but it was still cold and damp. A ridge of mountains stood off in the distance that looked like some kid had drawn them there with a pencil, and the sun was glazed and lying low.

"What's that?" I said.

"Walsh," he said.

"Who's Walsh?"

"Fellow that runs the station in Broke Creek, ain't you listening?"

"I'm trying to."

"Anyway, it's an odd situation and I just thought I'd warn you about it."

"You haven't said anything yet."

"I'm getting to it."

"Go ahead then."

In spite of trying to measure it, we'd already drunk down the schnapps and tossed the bottle off into the brush a long way back. I think I'd have broken a man's legs to get some more.

"This Walsh is a married fellow and has his wife there, working for him, and he's got a big nigger that works for him and some Mexican boy, too."

I shrugged.

"But he's also got this woman there, too . . . somebody he keeps for his pleasure. Her name's Sara something or other."

"I imagine it causes quite some dinner conversation," I said.

"I imagine so. But the thing I wanted to warn you is how jealous Walsh is of her. He nearly beat that Mexican kid who works for him to death over her. I'm surprised that the boy still works for him."

"Or hasn't cut his throat," I said.

"Or that," Burt said.

"I don't aim on making hay with somebody's woman," I said.

"I know it, but just so you know what the deal is."

"He must be something, this Walsh," I said.

"He acts like he is, but to me he's just a big blowhard bully."

"Let's whip his ass when we get there," I said.

"For what?"

"Pure principle."

Burt grinned. "We ought to, shouldn't we?"

"I was just kidding."

"It's a good idea."

"You do it then."

47

"I might."

"If he kills you, do I still get my money?"

"I'll have to check with the company, see how that works."

"Thanks," I said.

We made the last incline just as the sun winked out beyond the mountains and threw a fire up into the sky setting it momentarily ablaze. Below us we could see the station's buildings, all but one on the west side of a wide rippling creek. Every time I saw a tributary I was reminded all over again about the bear.

"That cabin sitting by itself," said Burt, "is the one the woman lives in. I'd stay shy of that cabin was I you."

Burt had to hold back the team on the descent and work the foot brake to keep the damned rig from getting out of control. He did it like he'd been doing it all his life and we soon enough hit level again.

But we didn't go far before we saw the body.

"That looks like the Mexican kid," Burt said, hauling back on the reins. The main house stood a hundred yards beyond. "Something's damn' wrong."

"Jealousy," I said.

"Maybe so, but why would Walsh leave him way out here? Why wouldn't he drop him down a well or something?"

I was already getting that old feeling coming

over me—the one that whispered danger in my ear.

"Let's just leave the stage here," Burt said, setting the foot brake and tying off the ribbons. He pulled his coat back and I saw what looked like a pearl-handled Merwin & Hulbert riding his hip bone.

I climbed down my side and Burt climbed down his. But I didn't wait for further instructions. I was already moving cautiously toward the house, the rabbit ear hammers of the 10-gauge thumbed back and set to go. Darkness was coming on fast now that the sun had set and even the shadows were being swallowed. I saw lights on inside the house.

I heard Burt saying something to the passengers behind me, but it wasn't until I heard another man's voice command him to throw his hands up that I turned to look over my shoulder in time to see the fancy-dressed dude step from the coach, a pistol in his hand aimed at Burt's head. I caught a glimpse of the woman, too. She was pointing a gun at the others that had stepped from the coach. Even the Chinaman had dropped down from the top.

I could have pulled the triggers on them but I would have had to have taken out Burt with them and I didn't want to risk that. Instead, I stayed to the shadows, moving toward the house, trying as I went to come up with some sort of plan. I was never one for plans. I most generally just did whatever needed doing.

The man and woman ordered Burt and the others to march toward the house. Voices carried at night more so than in the day, it seemed, like they do across water. I ducked into the shadows along one wall of the house, flattened myself against the wall, and waited.

The fancy-dressed man shouted at the house.

"Come on out, boys! I got these here, but there is another loose."

The door burst open and I heard boots clomping on the porch, men's voices asking: "Which way did he go, Davy?"

"Around there somewhere. Look for him, god damn it!"

It was dark and I didn't know how many were looking for me, but I started to move again, toward the open spaces beyond the house, figuring to get far enough away, then circle back around. Suddenly gunfire crackled in the dark like firecrackers set off and I dropped to the ground as bullets zipped the air overhead. I looked back and saw the muzzle flashes from their guns and pulled both triggers. Somebody screamed. I got up and kept running.

Then one of the gunmen yelled: "He shot Bob's arm off, Davy!"

"Well, go get the son-of-a-bitch before he shoots all your arms off!" came the reply.

50

"How we supposed to find him in this dark?"

I was moving away fast, then I stumbled into the creek, and the water was icy cold so that it felt like it burned. I gasped when I fell and nearly lost my grip on the 10-gauge, but rose again, and scrambled out the other side, breaking open the shotgun as I went, picking out the spent shells and replacing them with extras from my pockets.

I looked back again, couldn't see anyone against the skyline, no flashes of muzzle or sounds of gunshots. I think shooting Bob's arm off was just enough to make them think about coming after me in the dark. I know it would have me.

I moved toward the shape and shadow of the lone cabin, remembering what Burt had told me about the woman living there. It lay fifty yards or so directly across from the main house.

I came up silently on the back wall. It was crudely built, just curled unpainted boards chinked between. I remembered seeing a single window when we came down off the grade in the fading light. I moved around toward it, tried to look in, but the room was dark.

I heard something scratching, then a low moaning sound.

Across the creek I could see the lights from inside cast outward, see the outline of the coach, see the shadows of men, hear their voices.

"Where's the damn' key to unlock that strong-box?"

"Hell if I know," Burt's raspy voice said.

Then there was a bone-crunching sound followed by an utterance of someone in pain.

"I'm going to ask you again, but only one last time. Where's the damn' key?"

I heard Burt curse. "Screw you!" he said.

Then a gunshot and in that momentary flash I saw what had to be Burt collapse.

"Maybe you know now, you son-of-a-bitch," the voice said.

I slipped inside the cabin. Not surprisingly the door had no lock or bolt. I heard a sharp intake of breath, then the words: "Please don't hurt me no more please." A woman's voice.

"Hush," I said, crossing the space between me and her.

"Please!"

I reached out blindly and felt bare skin, felt her jerk back from my touch.

"I'm not here to do you any harm," I said in a low voice. "I need you to be quiet."

"They hurt me bad," she said.

"They'll not hurt you again," I said. "You got some clothes to put on?"

I felt her twist away and reach for something.

"Easy," I said.

"My shirt," she said.

I went back over and cracked the door wide enough to see across the creek. Heard the voices of frustrated men.

"What we goin' to do, Davy?"

"Get up in that driver's seat and let's get the hell going. Shoot these other sons-a-bitches."

Then there was a short silence before the gunfire crackled again, then more silence. I heard the crash of glass, then saw flames lifting up inside the house. They'd set it afire. The fire caught and spread quickly, probably because the house was old and the lumber dry, and the flames soon enough were licking at the black spaces around the house and throwing light into the yard. I saw men lying on the ground and knew one of them was my old friend.

Then the stage and the saddled horses with their riders rode out, leaving just the fire, the dead, me, and the woman.

"Wait here," I said to the woman.

She was still sobbing, a muted wounded sound.

I crossed over the footbridge, my clothes still wet and cold from falling into the creek earlier, but I didn't pay much attention to any of that. When you're in a fighting mode, you don't pay much attention to anything other than what you aim to fight.

I found Burt first and he was dead, and it pained me that he was.

I crossed the ground to the other three men. The Chinaman was also dead and so was the rancher with the peaked hat, both lying on their sides like they were sleeping and I guess they were—that eternal sleep we'll all take one day or another.

The last man I thought was dead, too, but, when I touched him, he groaned and sat up suddenly and said: "Jesus, I've been killed." He looked at me, then fell back. He was the one I'd taken for a gunfighter back at the ticket station.

I felt blood on the front of his shirt and he groaned, and I helped sit him up again.

"Can you stand?" I said.

"I don't rightly know."

"Can you try?"

"I reckon."

I helped him to his feet, and he stood, wobbling like a newborn colt.

The timber in the house cracked sharply, then the roof fell in, and minutes later the walls collapsed.

The woman had come from the cabin, dressed now in denims and a man's shirt and coat, her hair tied off with a length of ribbon. She was staring at the flames.

"Walsh," she said. Like it was the name of something. Only I knew it was the name of the stationmaster.

She pointed at the fire just as it started eating itself because it had nothing else to eat.

"Zelda," she said, her mouth agape.

I figured they were both inside but probably dead before the fire was set because I hadn't heard any screaming.

"Can you get some water and something to bind this man's wound?" I said. She looked at the shot man, and then went to the cabin and returned in minutes with both. She had him sit on the ground as she cleaned his wound.

"There's something in him," she said.

"Yeah, I figure it to be a bullet," he said.

"No, right here under the skin."

I went over and knelt, and sure enough the bullet was just under the skin, and I couldn't figure why it would be. Then he pulled back the lapel of his coat and I saw a dented badge and the light of the flames ran over it and exposed the words: *The Pinkerton Detective Agency.*

He fingered the badge. "For once this here did me some good," he said.

"I'm going to pluck that bullet out of you if you can stand it," I said. Then I asked the woman if she had some sort of knife, and she went to the cabin again and came back with a butcher knife, and the man looked at it and said: "That's a lot of knife."

I used the tip to pluck the lead slug out, and it was bloody and warm still.

"You might want to keep it for a good luck charm," I said.

He flung it away.

"I guess having a shotgun messenger didn't do much good this run," he said sourly.

"I guess having a Pinkerton detective on board

with the very man who shot you didn't do much good, either," I said.

The woman bound his wound as best she could, and we helped him to his feet again.

"Name's Dew Hardy," he said. "Pleased to make everyone's acquaintance." But there was no warmth behind the words.

The woman stood silently. The flames kept growing smaller. I knew I couldn't track them in the dark, and I knew I wanted to bury my friend. I knew I'd find them sooner or later and that I wouldn't stop looking until I did find them.

And I knew when I found them, I'd kill them.

Chapter Eight

By dawn I'd completed the back-breaking work of digging one large grave. I hated like hell to bury Burt that way, but I had no choice. The Pinkerton couldn't dig, and, although the woman tried, she couldn't get the spade through the cold rocky ground. I dug and took breaks and made myself a shuck and smoked, and then dug some more and kept at it.

At one point the woman asked if I'd make her a smoke and I did, and we sat and smoked together while the Pinkerton slept nearby.

"I don't know why they didn't kill me, too," she said.

"I don't know why, either," I said.

We sat and watched the flames go to embers.

"Walsh and Zelda was in that house," she said.

"I kind of figured they were," I said.

"I heard her screaming just before they came for me," she said.

I didn't want to talk about what they might have done and I don't think she did, either.

"I watched them beating Walsh in the yard while some of them were inside with Zelda," she said. "I tried to hide, but they found me and . . ."

"I was told there was a black man working here?"

"George," she said. "He run off."

She pointed toward the east.

"I wish he'd taken me with him," she said.

She sat with her knees pulled up, one arm wrapped around them as she smoked as though she was still trying to protect herself.

"I'm sorry for whatever they did to you," I said.

"Why should you be? You don't know me or nothing."

"I don't need to know somebody to feel sorry for them."

She looked at me strangely.

"I never have known anything but cruel men," she said.

"Maybe that will change," I said.

We smoked, then I went back to digging the grave.

Dawn broke—a seam of yellow light rimmed along the horizon. Then a bright orange sun lifted up and burned away the haze.

The Pinkerton roused from his sleep just as I was putting the bodies of Burt and the others into the big grave.

"I got to go off to that privy," he said.

"You don't need my permission," I said.

"I wasn't asking for it," he said.

The woman had gone back to the cabin for rest and was still there.

When the Pinkerton returned, he was carrying something in his right hand.

"Look what I found," he said. It was part of an arm with the hand—the one I'd shot off Bob.

"Get rid of it before the woman comes back," I said.

He tossed it into the smoldering ashes of the house, then said: "I saw a skull. There's body parts all over."

"Don't say anything about it to the woman," I said.

He sucked at his teeth, then looked down into the top of his shirt at the wound.

"It don't feel half bad," he said. "I never was shot before. I thought it would feel worse."

"Be glad it doesn't," I said, and put the last of the bodies—Burt's—into the grave next to the others, and started filling it in. The Pinkerton watched.

Then the woman came from the cabin; this time she wore a big felt hat and was carrying a carpetbag in her hand.

"I'm set to go," she said.

"Where?" I said.

"With you."

"Not with me," I said.

She looked to the Pinkerton. He shrugged, said: "Don't ask me nothing, lady."

"You're a son-of-a-bitch if you leave me here," she said to me. "You're no different than any of them who raped me. You might as well put a bullet in me."

I was exhausted from digging the grave, no sleep, anger, frustration. I didn't need a woman reminding me I wasn't the perfect man. I saw in her eyes the same thing I'd seen in my wife's the day I left the cabin to go find the bear. It pained me to see that look again.

"Fine," I said. "I'll carry you to the nearest settlement."

She didn't say anything.

I went to the horse shed and found an old spring wagon under the lean-to at the end, then roped two of the horses, and hitched them to the wagon. I helped the woman into the back along with her carpetbag. I supposed her only possessions were in that bag.

The Pinkerton climbed onto the seat next to me, and I took the reins after I rested the shotgun down under the seat and headed out toward the road and the direction the stage had gone.

"You know where the next station is?" I asked the woman over my shoulder.

"I don't know where nothing is," she said. "Walsh never took me nowhere but to my cabin."

"You ever hear of a town near here?"

"No," she said.

I looked at the Pinkerton. He'd seemed deep in thought.

"What about you?" I said. "You know this land?"

"Not much," he said.

"You ever track?"

"I can cut sign," he said.

"Good. Keep an eye out for that coach's wheels in case it turns off this road.

The sun was lifted, burning brightly over the pale green sage and chaparral, and the air was clean and cool but warming fast. And the mountains in the distance shimmered with fresh snow that had fallen up there overnight.

To look at it you could fall in love with that country. But it was a mean hard place for the unwary, and even for the wary it could be a mean hard place. I thought about the burned house and the skulls and the part arm and all the rest of what had happened in the last few hours, and it made me weary to think about it, and it made me want a drink worse than I ever wanted one.

"That fellow we're chasing," Dew Hardy said of a sudden.

"What about him?"

"I know who he is now."

"You want to share that information with me?"

He sort of half smiled but it wasn't from pleasure that he was smiling.

"Gypsy Davy," he said.

"Never heard of him."

"Well, I sure enough have. I've been dogging him for half a year now. That's why I'm in these parts . . . to find Gypsy Davy."

"It maybe would have been easier if you'd arrested him before he shot you," I said.

"I didn't recognize him. He dyed his hair yellow and grew that fancy Dan mustache and acted like a fairy. The Gypsy I heard of was always rough-and-tumble and wore a leather vest and leather britches and so forth. I never figured him to be a fancy Dan type."

"Don't they train you detectives?" I said.

"They do some, but rely most heavily on our *innate* skills."

"Innate?" I said.

"Why, yes."

"Maybe you ought to brush up on those innate skills then."

"And that woman," he said. "That had to have been Belle Moon, known associate of Davy's most recent. She used to run a whore house in

Creede, but I guess she's done gone to outlawing."

"I guess she has," I said. "Probably pays better and is less stressing on the flesh."

"Only if a body don't get shot doing their outlawing," he said.

"You'd be the expert on getting shot," I said.

"I reckon," he said.

"You two jabber like magpies," the woman said.

"Just what I need," I said. "Criticism."

We rode on. To what our destination was, I couldn't say, nor did I choose to guess. But whatever it turned out to be, I figured it would be short, violent, and bloody.

Chapter Nine

We followed the road for the next three hours until we came to another station set far back from the road. It wasn't dissimilar to the previous one except it wasn't burned to the ground and there weren't any dead bodies lying around.

I drove the team up to the main house.

There was a man in the corral, checking a horse's hoof, and another stood on the roof of the house with a hammer in his hand and a mouthful of nails.

A third man emerged from inside with a bandanna tucked into the top of his shirt and what looked like a half-eaten chicken leg in his hand. He had grease around his mouth and wore baggy, wrinkled trousers. His thick, rough shoes curled up at the toes and his ears stuck out like a baby elephant's.

"How-do," he said, and I returned the greeting. He looked at me first, then the Pinkerton, and then the woman. Especially at the woman. So, too, did the man standing on the roof, staring down at us, and the man in the corral who let the horse's hoof back down and straightened again. He might have been part Indian or Mexican judging by the color of his darker skin.

"Climb on down and stretch your legs," the man with the chicken leg said. The meat where he'd gnawed into it was pale and pink.

We climbed down, and I asked the man, could we water the horses, and he said—"Yes, help yourself"—and pointed with the drumstick toward a water tank near the corral, and I led the team over and let them drink.

The man followed us over but his interest was all about the woman.

"The Deadwood to Cheyenne stage come through here recent?" I said.

He nodded.

"Way off schedule," he said.

"You notice anything unusual?" I said.

"Different driver than usual," he said. "Usually it's Burt Bee whipping the horses."

"Burt Bee's dead," I said. "Killed last night at the Broke Creek station."

The man bit off another piece of his chicken, chewed it slowly, still looking at the woman. "No shit?" he said.

"Killed Burt and the stationmaster, his wife, the Mexican boy, and some of the passengers. Made off with the strongbox."

The man scratched his chin whiskers, rubbed the grease from his mouth with his fingertips, and looked at them.

"That's hard news."

"You got somebody here can ride to Deadwood and let them know?"

He turned and looked at the man in the corral.

"Reckon I could send Frank."

"Then please do," I said.

"What about you-all?" he said.

"I'd like to leave the woman here until somebody can come for her. Me and this man are in pursuit of those on that stage."

He swallowed hard like a piece of that chicken was stuck in his throat and his eyes grew moist with the desire for her.

"That'd be peaches," he said. Then to the woman: "You was Walsh's woman, wasn't you?"

She gave him a hard glare. The man on the roof hadn't moved.

"I wasn't nobody's woman," she sad.

The old man held up the hand with the chicken leg.

"My apologies, I thought you was."

Then to me she said: "I'm not staying with this old coot and them others."

"I don't reckon you have any choice," I said.

"Why is me coming with you a bother?"

"You'll just slow us down."

"Slow you down? You think me riding in that damned wagon is somehow going to slow you down?"

"I aim to ask this man to lend us some saddle horses," I said, and turned to the man to ask him just that.

"Sorry," he said, "I got none I can lend you. These horses is all company horses for the stages."

"We just need two," I said.

He shook his head.

"How about the use of some saddles, then. We'll saddle the two I got hitched to the wagon."

He turned and called to the man on the roof.

"Jake, you want to lend this man your saddle?"

"Hell no!" Jake shouted. I couldn't be sure if he was smiling or not.

"Frank, you want to lend these fellows your saddle?"

"Not on my worst day!" Frank called from the corral.

The old man shrugged.

"Whisht I could help you out, but thems the only two who own a saddle 'round here. I quit horseback riding when I turned seventy."

Then he gnawed the meat of his chicken leg down to the bone and gnawed the bone and then sucked on it before tossing it aside.

"I got a nice extra room you can stay in, miss," he said. He was practically slobbering on himself, looking at her.

"You'd have to shoot me first," she said without pleasure. Then she looked at me, too, as though the statement was made for both of us and not just that old lecher.

"Where's the nearest town from here?" I asked.

He looked off and pointed toward a flat valley.

"Beyond there," he said. "Two Cents."

"That's the name of the town . . . Two Cents?"

"I know it," he said. "But that's about all it's worth and that's what ever'body calls it. Two Cents."

"How far?" I said.

"Twenty miles or so."

"How do we get there?"

"Up the same road you was on about two miles, then turn off it and follow that other 'un the rest of the way."

"Let's go," I said to the Pinkerton and the woman.

She didn't even bother to say thank you. I guess I couldn't blame her.

"When we get there," I said as I started off toward the road again, "you're staying there, no more arguments."

She gave me one of those assassin stares.

Chapter Ten

We found the Deadwood stage where the road toward Two Cents came in from the west. We found bodies, too. The stage doors were wide open, the horses gone, and the dead had each been shot in the back of the head. One of them was missing an arm that had been crudely bandaged, the bandages crusted with blood.

"What do you figure happened here?" the Pinkerton said as we cautiously climbed down.

There were three of them. Men still wearing pistol belts but their pistols were gone.

"My guess is they're part of your man's gang," I said.

Dew Hardy went over and more closely examined each of them, worked his hands through their pockets.

"That part of your job?" I said. "Robbing the dead?"

"It's called investigation," he said.

"So you say," I said.

A wheel of buzzards, their dark bodies turning against the sky, had already sniffed out the tragedy and were waiting for a feast. Dew Hardy saw them, too.

"The Lord does provide," he said with an ugly smile before continuing to search the men.

The woman sat silently in the back of the wagon, staring at them, then she climbed down and came over to look as Dew Hardy turned them onto their backs to have a go through their front pockets.

"That one was one of them," she said, then spat on his dead face.

"Enough," I said, and stepped between her and the bodies.

"He hurt me," she said. "And so did these others."

She was mad as hell and in a way I couldn't blame her.

I walked the trail back and forth and saw three sets of horse tracks leading off down the road to Two Cents. I saw some other tracks leading down into the nearby arroyo, figured they were part of the team cut loose from the stage and set free. Odd that a man would kill his companions but set horses free. But then nothing made any real sense to me any more.

"They went this way," I said, pointing up the road.

Dew Hardy had taken from the dead men a total of one pocket watch, two clasp knives, an Indian head penny, and a deck of dog-eared playing cards.

"They didn't leave this world with much more than what they had when they came into it," he said.

"You don't call that robbing?" I said.

"Somebody would have searched them and taken what they had," he said.

"Leave it," I said.

He looked at the paltry bounty, then at me, then at it again.

"Hell," he said, and tossed the few items down.

"Let's go," I said.

"We could be riding straight into a trap," he said. "There must be a reason for them to go this way."

"Or maybe they're just trying to get the hell gone and this was the way to go," I said.

"Davy's a real sly buck," he said.

"I reckon he thinks we're dead," I said.

"Maybe so."

"Let's go," I said again.

We headed off to Two Cents. It took half a day to get there, but when we topped a rise, we saw the collection of buildings down below that looked enough to be a town but not much of one.

We paused long enough to study on it, then I drove the team down to it.

Two Cents was just a crossroads mostly with a road running north and south and one running east and west—both meandering and cut like a brown scar on the earth. A river of no important size rippled along the east-west road and disappeared in both distances and maybe that's what started the town—its ready supply of water—or it might have been the mines I saw on the hills above the town with their piles of tailings sloping down the hillsides.

We rode in and I figured we best eat something since we hadn't for some time. I was starved and I figured the woman was, too.

I stopped the wagon across the street from a building simply marked *RESTAURANT* and we went in and found a table near one wall and sat. Over our heads was a large cardboard print of a sprawling battle between Indians and soldiers that read:

Custer's Last Fight
ANHEUSER-BUSCH BUDWEISER

The boy wonder stood in the middle with his sword raised, fighting off the swarming horde of Sioux. Trouble was none of those boys ever took swords with them into the fight the way I heard it. Still, it made for a dramatic scene, one that would stir the blood of young men anxious to go and kill off the last red man that ever was.

"I bet he made a pretty corpse," Dew Hardy said, looking up at it.

We ate our meal without humor. Nobody wanted to think more about corpses. Seemed to me the earth had soaked up as much blood as it could hold.

After we finished, Dew Hardy said: "Where do you propose we begin looking for Davy and Belle?"

"You're the detective," I said, "skilled in such matters. Where do you propose we begin?"

"I say we go and check in with the local law if there is any and ask him."

"Sounds like a capital idea," I said. "But I want to get her settled into a room."

The woman looked at me.

"Why don't I settle her into a room and *you* go ask the law?" Dew Hardy said.

"You always so damn' disagreeable about everything?" I said.

"Mostly, yes," he said.

We paid our bill and walked outside. I could see the eyes of men watching us from under their hat brims, and even the few women that were out and about, walking the plank board-walks, gave us stares. We were strangers and it wasn't unusual to keep an eye on strangers and, I reckon, we were an odd-looking trio, me, Dew Hardy, and the woman—all three of us muddy and looking run over as we were.

I saw a hotel sign up the street.

"I'll meet you out front of that hotel in twenty minutes," I said to Dew Hardy.

"Fine," he said, and stalked off.

Sara got her carpetbag from the back of the wagon, and I walked her over to the hotel.

A skinny fellow stood behind the desk and his hands shook almost as much as mine were beginning to without having had a drink for however long it had been. He had a high, thin, nervous voice: "Can I help you two?"

"I'd like a room for the lady?"

He sort of laughed and his laughter sounded sort of like a strange bird—one of those sandhill cranes from a long distance.

"Sure, sure," he said, and asked her to sign the register, and then said: "For how long . . . just the afternoon?" Then he looked at me like I knew something only the two of us knew and we weren't about to tell anybody.

"For two weeks," I said. Then I looked at Sara. "Do you think two weeks will be enough for you to find some work and get settled in?"

"How the hell should I know," she said.

"Well, nothing like a show of gratitude to make a fellow feel good," I said.

"Ten dollars and that's with the long-term discount," the fellow said. Come to think of it, the more I looked at him the more he looked like a sandhill crane.

I paid him out of the advance that Burt had given me.

"You want a room overlooking the street or somewhere in the back?" he asked Sara.

"Overlooking the street," she said.

He reached in a cubbyhole and took out a key

and said: "Room Ten, up the stairs and second door on your right."

I carried her bag up for her. It wasn't a fancy hotel, but it wasn't a pigsty, either. It had carpet on the stairs, although worn and stained with mud and tobacco juice. The stairs squeaked when we climbed them.

She unlocked the door and we went in and the room was full of light from a floor-to-ceiling window. She went to it and looked down. I put the carpetbag on the bed.

"You all set?" I said.

"I've got a few dollars I saved up . . . my sugar money," she said.

"Sugar money?"

"I always thought someday I'd buy myself passage somewhere . . . to a sugarland of a place and find true happiness," she said. "So I saved up every cent I could." She patted one of the pockets of her trousers.

"Well, I'd hardly say that Two Cents looks like a sugarland, but it has to beat hell out of that station."

She looked at me oddly then and came and stood close to me.

"You can stay if you like," she said.

"I've got to find those two killers," I said.

"You look wore out," she said.

"I am."

"Then stay, at least tonight. And if you

decide to leave tomorrow, then let it be tomorrow."

"I thought maybe by now you'd had enough of men," I said.

She stared hard into my eyes.

"Certain kind of men, yes," she said. "But I've not known many men with a kindness about them like you."

"Nothing kind about me," I said. "I'm just a man looking to drink himself into a grave and kill a few people before I do it. You call that kind?"

She put her hand on my arm.

"You wouldn't be killing nobody without reason," she said.

"How do you know that?"

"I just know. I got a good sense about people."

"I'd trade you for a bottle right now," I said.

"No. You wouldn't," she said.

"I might."

She kissed me suddenly and I had almost known she would do it, but I didn't kiss her back because I knew how easily I could give myself to her and I knew that, if I did, it wouldn't be the right thing for either of us.

When she finished and drew back, she said: "Is it because of what those men did to me?"

"Don't be crazy," I said. "It ain't got nothing to do with you."

"Then what?"

"I can't explain it."

She turned and walked to the window again, the light glowing around her in a strange sort of way.

"I'll be here if you change your mind," she said. "Thank you for helping me."

I turned and walked out and back down the stairs, and, as I passed the front desk, the crane said to me: "My that was quick."

I stopped and looked at him.

"Anything happens to that woman," I said, "I'll take it real personal."

His gaze dropped to the shotgun.

"Yes, sir," he said, or maybe it was a birdcall, I couldn't rightly tell.

I waited out front of the hotel. I made myself a shuck but spilled half the tobacco doing it. I needed a drink badly. I thought I'd smoke and wait for Dew Hardy until I couldn't wait any longer. It didn't take long.

Just about every other door along the street was a saloon, and I went into the first one I came to and walked down to the far end of the bar. Eyes watched me. The place was long and narrow and the air was smoky from men's cigars. Voices that were talking to each other momentarily paused in order for them to study me.

I took up residence and set the shotgun atop the wood. The old man tending bar had a hairless skull but a mustache like bicycle handles. He walked down and I ordered whiskey. "Make it quick," I told him, and he poured, then stood and watched as I tossed it back. Then he said: "You want another?"

"Of course," I said, and he poured another.

"You got it bad, don't you?" he said.

I stared at him.

"I ain't judging you, mister," he said. "I've been there myself and know what it's like. Have another." He poured. "This one is on the house."

I nodded and with the third one tossed back my nerves started to settle some. Those along the bar had stopped watching and had gone back to their intimate conversations about the weather, the mines, women, horses.

I stood apart from them, and they from me, and that was the way I preferred it. I didn't trust anyone, not even a woman who was willing to give herself to me because that's how I had grown since it'd happened. . . .

The barkeep left the bottle as he tended to business farther down the bar, and I poured myself another, and this time just stared into it, seeing some of my own reflection.

You're a damned boozer, I told myself. *You've crawled into the bottle and into the bottle is where you'll die.*

I lifted the glass to my lips and drank.

Chapter Eleven

I walked back to the hotel and waited. Again I rolled myself a shuck but my hands didn't spill as much tobacco. Passers-by still looked at me oddly, at the shotgun leaning against the wall by my right leg. I didn't much care.

Finally Dew Hardy came swinging up the street.

"You find the law?" I said.

He snorted. "Not exactly but I did find somebody told me the marshal was away fishing. You think it might have something to do with Gypsy and Belle being around . . . that the only law this dog-shit town has is away fishing?"

"Sounds suspicious," I said. "What do you think our next move should be, detective?"

He looked at me, then at the entry to the hotel.

"You get her settled in nice and proper?" It wasn't a question born out of concern as much as it was suspicion.

"She's settled," I said.

"Be best if we split up and went separate ways looking for them," he said.

"It wouldn't be because you'd like to get that gold for yourself, would it?"

"Hell, no denying I would."

"Well, at least you're honest about it. But I'm not going to let you take that gold," I said.

"So's you can keep it for yourself? You and her maybe?" he said, looking at the hotel door again.

"Because I aim to take it back to Deadwood and give it to those who own it."

He looked at me like I'd just stepped on his toes.

"Shit, I'm like old Diogenes," he said. "Still looking for one honest man."

"Why am I not surprised you've read the classics?" I said.

"Why ain't I surprised you even know about the classics?" he said.

"OK," I said. "We'll split up and meet back here in a few hours."

"I might not learn anything till the night comes and men's tongues get loose with liquor." he said.

"Then tomorrow morning first thing," I said.

"Sounds like an ace plan."

He went his way, I went mine.

The first place I checked was the livery.

A man in a shiny bowler and dress shoes sat out front on a wood bench with a pitchfork in one hand, looking defeated. His dress shoes were mucked up. I could hear horses snuffling in the shadows.

"Help you?" he said.

"I'd like to look over your horseflesh," I said.

"You a buyer?"

"Yes," I lied.

"Well now," he said.

He stood with a hopeful look in his round little face and offered me his hand to shake and I shook it. It was small and soft and damp.

"You mind if I wander through your barn and take a look at what you have?"

"Be my guest. Where'd you say you were from?"

"Cheyenne," I said. Another lie.

"Cheyenne, eh?"

I entered the barn and it smelled of hay and horse. A blade of light ran down the center from the front to the back door. I checked each stall for a branded horse—one that would have the mark of the stage line. I found it on a blaze-faced sorrel.

I turned to the little fellow who trailed me, hopeful.

"This one," I said.

"Yes, sir, fine horse, real fine horse."

"How'd you come by him?"

The little fellow shrugged. "Honestly I can assure you about him."

"I'd like to see the papers on him."

The little fellow looked nervous.

"Well, they sort of got lost."

I shifted my shotgun from cradling it to one hand.

"This one is stolen," I said.

"Oh, no, sir."

"He's got a brand on his flank. He came off a robbed stage."

He stammered and shuffled his feet.

"I wouldn't know anything about it," he said. "I wasn't here when the horse came in."

"Who *was* here when he came in?"

"Glen Weaver, my hired hand."

"Where is he now?"

He shrugged.

"He quit on me yesterday."

"Why is that?"

"I don't know. I just come to check on things and he was gone. It's hard to keep anybody working mucking out stalls, that's why I'm doing it myself . . . till I can hire a new man."

"How can I find Glen Weaver?" I said.

"I guess at home," he said.

"Where is his home?"

He drew me a map on how to get to Glen Weaver's place.

"Honest, mister, I didn't know nothing about that horse being stolen. I'm an honest man."

"Honest, huh? Maybe you ought to tell that to Dew Hardy. He's been looking for an honest man."

"Who's Dew Hardy?"

I drove the wagon out to Glen Weaver's place as described by the rough map. It sat back off the road a few hundred yards—just an old log cabin with some crude out buildings, something of a corral, and what looked like an old pigsty but without any pigs in it—just the mud wallow.

A pack of dogs came baying and barking out

from the house and spooked the horses so they nearly ran off with me. I fired one of the barrels into the air and that spooked them again, but it also spooked the dogs and they ran back toward the house.

A woman and three kids stood there in front of the house by the time I tied off and got out of the wagon. They looked unwashed and worn grim. It was hard to say how old the woman might have been but those kids couldn't have been more than ten or twelve, the oldest of them. All tow-headed boys.

"I'm looking for Glen Weaver," I said. "Is this his place?"

"Who are you?" she said.

"It doesn't matter who I am. Where is he at?"

"He ain't here."

"You mind if I go in and take a look?"

"Yes," she said.

I went past her and stepped into the low-ceiling cabin. There were pallets on the floor, an old wood stove, a dry sink, and not much else. It smelled of cooking grease. Out back there was a handmade table and a couple of chairs standing in what could loosely be described as a yard. There was a pump, and off a way stood a privy. It was bare-bones living.

"Where'd he go?" I said when I stepped back out front again.

She looked pitiful over the question. Her boys

stood wide-eyed with grim faces, bowl haircuts, and jug ears.

"Some man came and took him," she said.

"Took him? Took him where?"

She pointed off toward the chaparral.

"Yonder," she said.

Her lips quivered, remembering.

"He come, and another, and they called him from the house, saying they would burn it unless he come out. They asked him where the money was and he said he didn't know nothing about any money, and they said they'd shoot me and our youngsters unless he told them. So he said it was in the privy." She pointed. "Then they told him to go get it, and he come back with some saddlebags, and he gave it to them. Then the man swung a rope over Glen and they dragged him off through the brush."

"Was the other one a woman?" I said.

"I don't know," she said. "It was dark. They was both dressed like men, but I don't know."

The direction she pointed looked rugged, too much so for a wagon.

"You have a saddle around here anywhere?" I said.

She nodded.

"Tad, go get papa's saddle from 'round back."

The tallest of the boys ran off as I unhitched a horse from the wagon. He came back lugging an old Army saddle.

"Ask your ma if she has a canteen I can take, and put some water in it."

He went and returned with a clay jug with a stopper and a piece of rope around its neck I could hook onto the saddle. I've ridden harder things, but I couldn't remember when. I started off in the direction the woman had pointed and rode for maybe a mile or two up and down over the caliche-covered hills and across little arroyos following the drag marks, bits of clothing, blood, until I found Glen Weaver.

He was lying there, twisted, and I thought he was dead until I came near and saw the slight rise and fall of his chest. His flesh was all torn and bloody, and flies swarmed over the wounds of his face, arms, and legs. Even his feet were a mess.

I unhooked the water jug and knelt by him and swiped the flies off before I shaded his face with my hat.

"Mister Weaver," I said. "Can you hear me?"

He groaned. I spilled some water over his face and mouth.

His one eye opened; the other was swollen shut or missing, I couldn't tell which.

"Shoot me," he said.

"I can't do that," I said.

"Please, God, please."

I judged his one leg to be broken pretty badly and maybe one of his arms as well.

"I'm killed anyway," he uttered.

"I told your wife I'd find you," I said.

He rolled his gaze away from me, then back again, the eye staring at me like something evil or haunting.

"I ain't no good this way," he said. "You got any mercy, you'll shoot me."

I stood away then, picking up the shotgun I'd laid next to him. He was right that he wouldn't last the trip back even if I had a way to get him back other than slung over the horse. We'd go back in the dark with me walking, and I'd have done it if that's all it was. But he was finished. It was just a matter of whether I wanted to leave him here to die slowly or sooner.

His eye kept staring at me. I couldn't just walk away and leave him like that and I couldn't just squat and watch him die slowly, either.

"You sure?" I said.

He nodded, and closed the eye. I pulled the trigger.

I rode back to the house.

"You find Glen?" the woman said.

"I did, yes, ma'am."

I didn't have to tell her the outcome since Glen wasn't with me.

She just stood there and nodded once.

"I carried rocks and put them over him. It was all I could do."

"You want to stay to supper?" she asked.

"No, ma'am, I got to be getting back," I said, unsaddling the horse and hitching it back up to the wagon.

"I appreciate you going to look for Glen," she said.

I didn't say anything. I could still see that eye watching me, afraid of what was, afraid of what was to be. I couldn't blame him, either way. I wondered if in those final moments he thought about whether all the money in all the world was worth the price he'd have to pay to try and get rich. But then I imagined most men wondered the same thing at one time or another.

Chapter Twelve

It was a long dreary trip back to Two Cents. The dark descended upon the world and the taste in my mouth was bad, like blood.

I saw the lights of the town twinkling out in front of me in the dark and was glad to see them. I was hungry and tired and thirsty. I was weary of the chase, and, if it hadn't been for my obligation to bring about justice for Burt, I'd probably have quit the trail then and there, gone in and gotten dead drunk, and kept on drifting until death itself found me, or I it.

I halted the wagon in front of the first saloon I came to and went in. The place was small and narrow, like most of them. Yellow light glowed off the tin ceiling and smoked swirled in the air. Talk was a rumble of voices, all mixed together with the clack of a wheel of fortune and the faro dealer's call.

I took up residence at the bar's end, as was my custom, so I could watch the front door to see who might come in—maybe a fancy-dressed man with a good-looking, highbrow lady. I ordered my usual, a bottle of whiskey, not the best, but not the worst, either. I couldn't afford the best and you never want to drink the worst unless you have to because of the headaches it'll give you. The worst stuff they call forty-rod, or snakehead. It's for wild kids who want to get drunk cheap their first time, and old-timers who want to get drunk their last time.

The barkeep was a skinny man with his dark wet hair combed straight forward and scissored off straight across his forehead. He reminded me of somebody I knew sometime but I couldn't remember who or where or when. He had long thin fingers and wore a gold signet ring on the pinky of his right hand. He looked at me and said: "You look familiar."

"You do, too."

"Where you hail from?"

"Here, there," I said.

"Didn't mean to pry," he said.

"No offense taken."

"I used to teach school up in Red Lodge," he said. "Montana Territory."

"I know where it is," I said.

He wiped a wet spot on the wood with the rag he took from over his left shoulder.

"My late wife was from up around there," I said, tossing back my drink and pouring myself another.

"That so? What was her name?"

"Ophelia Carson," I said.

"I was at your wedding," he said. "I'm Ophelia's cousin, Roy Tender. We didn't hardly meet except that once."

He extended his hand and I shook it.

"How'd she die?" he said. "I mean I heard rumor she had, but that was a while back and I'd already moved over this way. I lost track of her people."

I told him she died of the consumption. It wasn't anybody's business what she died of. It didn't matter.

He shook his head and his face grew grim.

"Awfully young to die of anything," he said.

He reached under the bar and got a glass and started to reach for a bottle on the shelf behind him.

"I'd like to drink to her memory," he said.

I poured him one from my bottle instead.

"Here's to Ophelia," he said, raising his glass. I didn't feel much like talking about her, but I clinked glasses with him anyway. He licked his lips.

"That bottle's on me," he said, pointing at the one we'd been drinking from.

"I don't need the charity," I said.

"Not offering any. Let it be some small comfort to you if it may. I don't know what else to do or say."

"Thanks, Roy," I said. He smiled and went back to work, to the men clamoring for more liquor, cursing about anything that troubled their minds, those hungry, sad, lonely, drunk men who found it necessary to drink every night in a den amongst each other. Maybe some of them had wives to go home to and that was part of the problem, or maybe they didn't have anything but an empty room and empty bed awaiting them and that was also part of the problem. I just knew I didn't have either. I tossed back another drink, corked the bottle, and walked out into the night air.

It was raining a nice soft gentle rain.

I'd been thinking about Sara ever since she offered herself to me. I knew it was wrong. I knew nothing about her and she knew nothing about me, except right then we were just two lonely souls looking for something even if we didn't know what it was.

I looked across the street at the hotel, the red brick dark now from the wetness. My gaze went up to the second story where I saw her light was still on, and I succumbed to the temptation.

She answered the door almost before I finished knocking and wordlessly stepped aside to let me in. I didn't say anything, but instead leaned the shotgun against the wall, then removed my hat and slapped the rain from it against my leg before turning to face her.

For a long time neither of us spoke—what was wanted, or what was not. She was dressed in a dark blue silk kimono.

"I'm glad you changed your mind," she said.

I put the bottle on a chair by the bed, and then sat myself on the bed's edge and pulled off my boots and socks. She watched me carefully.

"I probably could stand a bath," I said.

"You talk too much about other things," she said.

"I don't know what else to talk about any more."

She came and held forth her arms and hands as though inviting a child and I stood and she lifted my shirt over my head and then undid my belt and I stepped out of my jeans. She pressed herself against me and her body was warm and soft and I sensed something in it wanting just as my own body wanted.

Her head tilted up and her eyes shone in the soft light like wet stones. Her mouth was soft and yielding against mine. Her tongue flicked against my lips like a darting minnow before I let it into the cave of my mouth. My mind went numb against everything but her, us, that moment, and I did not think of the past or of the future, only of the moment. And I did not think of her, either, of her past. It didn't matter. Nothing mattered.

The wind blew the rain now against the window glass and thunder shook through the room followed by a bright bolt of lightning that lit us up like a photographer's flash. She had let the kimono drop away and stood naked, her flesh pale and bruised from the men who had abused her.

I wanted desperately to stand between her and any more pain, to become her protector forever more. It was not love in my heart for her, but something other than love that I could not explain even to myself—those things I was feeling as we toppled onto the bed.

She wrapped herself about me and we clung to each other against the storm's rage and lost ourselves in it and in one another.

Later we laid side-by-side, she curled against me.

"You make love like you're angry at me," she said.

"I'm sorry," I said.

"It is OK. I'm kind of used to it."

"Please, don't talk about anything in the past," I said. "I'm not one of those men."

"I know you ain't, Royce."

She stood from the bed and walked naked to the window and looked through its rain-streaked glass.

"Will you make us cigarettes?" she said over her shoulder.

"Yes."

I leaned out of the bed and got the makings from my coat pocket and fashioned us each a shuck and lit them. My fingers shook a little but I had what was left in the bottle to solidify me against the tremors I knew would get worse.

She turned from the window and came to the bed and took the cigarette I lit for her. She put it to her lips and stared down at me, the glow from her smoke flaring each time she drew on it.

"Come, sit down," I said.

I saw in her sad, hungry eyes the face of a woman who knew there was too little hope left for her and nowhere to turn any more. She seemed most vulnerable to me.

"I was hoping you'd change your mind," she said, sitting down then. "I'm really glad you did."

"I didn't plan on it," I said. "It just happened. I want you to know that."

"Don't matter whether you did or not. I'm just glad you came back."

"I don't want you to think . . ."

She shushed me by putting her fingers against my lips.

"Let's just enjoy each other tonight and let the tomorrows take care of themselves, OK?"

I nodded. She was right. To hell with tomorrows.

She was surprisingly loving with me—gentle and genteel. I tried not to think of the brutality wrought against her by other men. I wondered why she even trusted me or any man.

"Did you find them?" she said after a time.

"No."

"I wish you had . . . not on my account, but because of your friend. The ones who hurt me . . . well, at least they're dead and good riddance."

"I had to shoot a man," I said, swinging around on my side of the bed, reaching for the bottle, then letting it be. "Earlier."

She remained quiet.

"He was dying and begged me to do it."

Her hand touched my shoulder, her mouth pressed against my back. Again I was surprised at the effect such tenderness had on me.

"This fellow had a wife and several children," I said. "Now, she has no man, those kids no daddy."

"It wasn't your fault," she whispered, her breath warm against my skin, her breath smoky.

"I couldn't save him."

"You did him a kind act then."

"I surely could stand a drink," I said, and reached for the bottle and this time took hold of it.

"Wait," she said.

She rose again from the bed and crossed the room to the carpet-sided bag that contained her possessions and took out a small tin whose metal winked in the next flash of lightning and brought it to the bed, climbed in next to me.

"Take some of these," she said, pressing some small pills into my palm.

"What are they?"

"Cocaine pills. They'll settle your nerves. Better than whiskey," she said. "But better with the whiskey."

I washed them down with a long pull from the bottle, and she did, too.

We finished our smokes and laid back on the bed again.

"What's worse, do you suppose," I said, "a boozer or a dope fiend?"

She laughed.

"It don't matter, does it, Royce? We all have our crutches in life . . . booze, pills, sex. Whatever gets us through the night, I reckon."

"I reckon so, too," I said.

We made love again, only the second time I felt myself enveloped in a slow, peaceful haze that at some point felt as if we'd become one body, me and her, a single being that sought to exhaust itself upon itself and only then, when it finally did, did we fall unashamedly asleep.

I dreamed that night of Glen Weaver looking

at me with one eye, saying: *Please take my life, mister . . . it ain't worth nothing this away.*

Then the gun went off in my hand in a loud crash that woke me only to realize it was a clap of thunder and not a pistol shot. There was no one there but Sara, and I closed my eyes again and fell back into the same dream.

Chapter Thirteen

The next thing that awakened me wasn't thunder but something like it.

The door crashed in and a shadow stood framed in it.

"You looking for me, you son-of-a-bitch!"

I reached for my shotgun, then remembered it was on the far wall. Bullets slammed into me like bare-knuckle fists knocking all the air out of me. I reached for Sara. But then my world went dark.

When I opened my eyes again, the room was white, smelled medicinal. I tried to sit up but it was if heavy sharp rocks were lying on my chest. I fell back trying to decipher it all.

A woman in a high-collar dress came and stood next to my bed. She wore a white pinafore over a gray dress. She had an angel's face with pale blue eyes, a scarf covered her head, but a few sprigs of hair the color of ripened wheat had freed themselves from under the scarf's edge.

"Don't try and move," she said. "You've been terribly wounded."

My thoughts were as scattered as pieces of a jigsaw puzzle that have been kicked off a table.

My throat was so parched I could barely swallow and my tongue was scratchy against the roof of my mouth. She poured me a cup of water from a pitcher, and then put one hand under my head, tilting it upward so that I could drink.

"Slowly," she said. "Not too much now." She had an Irish brogue.

The water was not cold but it tasted like salvation, and I tried to get more of it before she pulled it away.

"You can't drink too much," she said. "You've chest wounds, so you must be careful."

I had a mind full of questions that needed answers, but before I could get any of them asked, I sank into the darkness again. And when I opened my eyes later, the long room with beds lined up either side was dim and nearly dark. I could hear the groans of men, could smell the smells of sickness and all that goes with sickness.

It went on and on like that—waking up and going under again—for what seemed like forever. Sometimes the blue-eyed woman would be there, and sometimes another, and sometimes a fellow with silver hair and mustaches. They'd roll me over and change the bedding and give me water and sometimes soup to swallow. I wanted to scream that I couldn't breathe, that everything inside me felt broke. But I couldn't and I didn't.

Then I started to remember the shadow in the doorway of the room and about Sara and what had led up to that moment and what the man had said: *You looking for me you son-of-a-bitch*. Then nothing until I woke in the white room.

Days passed and I slowly started to put things together. I had learned that the man with the silver mustaches and hair was a doctor and that the women were nuns and the place was a Catholic infirmary somewhere a few miles from town.

I learned some of this from a big black man who looked like a giant and had a head full of hair like cotton waiting to be picked. His name he said was Lincoln Johnson and that he was an orderly.

He was soft-spoken and deep-voiced. He helped me from my bed to the privy and back again and got me water and brought me trays of food once I could eat solids and keep them down. He asked me if I liked sitting in the sunshine and fresh air, and I said that I did, and he helped me go outside where I eased down into a wood rocker beneath a big cottonwood whose trunk was smooth as bone and spotted green and ivory.

"I sure could use a drink of something," I said when I got up the courage.

"You shake in your sleep," he said. "I seen you do it."

"Nightmares," I said.

"You got the whiskey fever," he said. "Had a brother who caught it, too. It killed him. They found him this one time sitting in a snowbank with a half-drunk bottle of snakehead liquor clutched in his hand. I had to go up there and get him and bring him home to his mama so we could bury him proper and the preacher could pray over him. You got the whiskey fever."

"I still could use a drink," I said.

"We all could use something or other," he said, and looked off toward the road that ran past the place like a wide brown scar that could be seen through the arched entry of a whitewashed wall of plaster that encircled the infirmary. Others sat out in the compound, too. Some of them dozed in their wheelchairs and others stared startle-eyed off into nothing at all. Some limped on crutches, and for others didn't seem like there was anything wrong with them.

The nuns went about speaking to them, reading to them, writing letters for some of them.

"These are some kind people," I said.

"They good people, sure enough," Lincoln said. Then: "I's the one found you out on that road yonder. Thought you was dead. Butt naked like the day you was born and bleeding. I saw you and thought . . . Lord, how'd this body show up here of a sudden? Then I seen your fingers twitch and knew they wasn't any dead man twitched his fingers."

"I don't remember much of it," I said, "except the shadow of a man in my doorway one night."

"Well, he shot you good. Three times and I never did know any man who got shot three times and lived, though three is a lucky number some say."

"Nobody who's ever been shot three times would say it was a lucky number," I said.

"Reckon it depends on how you look at it."

"There was a woman I was with that night," I said.

"There always is when it comes to bad troubles between mens."

"No, I don't think he shot me because of her."

"Why do you think he shot you, then?"

"Because he knew I was looking for him," I said.

"Why was you looking for him, you don't mind my asking?"

"He killed a friend of mine and I aimed to repay the favor."

"He sounds like a killing fool, for he done nearly killed you, too."

"Nearly ain't close enough," I said. "You got makings I could roll myself a shuck with?"

"I wish I could help you out, but I don't smoke," he said. "I doubt you could roll yourself a carpet the way you shake. I don't have the habit, but maybe . . ."

"That's OK," I said, but my nerves felt like freshly strung wire singing in the wind.

"I gots to go back to work," he said. "Just flag me down when you want to go back inside."

I thanked him and watched him lumber off. He moved slow, like he was carrying a great weight on his shoulders, and I figured he probably was in one way or another given his age and what all he'd seen and been through.

Then Sister Margaret came round the corner and she was carrying a small book in her hands and she sat next to me and said: "How are you doing today, Mister Blood?"

"How do you even know my name?" I said.

"Why you told it to me, don't you remember?"

"I tend to forget certain things, then they come to me, and then they go away again."

"It's probably the trauma of being shot nearly dead," she said. "Who could blame you?"

Somewhere a bird sang way up in the branches of the cottonwood that allowed the sun to filter down and fall like patterns of lace upon the ground.

"You need a shave, Mister Blood."

"I'd just as soon let my beard grow," I said.

"It's unsanitary," she said.

"Not if I wash it good."

She nodded her head gently as though she understood she couldn't win that particular case with me.

"Would you like me to read to you a bit?" she said.

"Sure," I said.

She opened the book.

"Anything in particular?" she said.

"Whatever strikes your fancy, Sister, I'm not choosy."

She looked at me with an arched brow.

"Just pick something at random," I said.

"OK."

She started to read: " 'And it came to pass in an evening tide, that David arose from off his bed, and walked upon the roof of the king's house, and from the roof he saw a woman washing herself; and the woman was very beautiful to look upon.' " She paused.

"Go on," I said. "It sounds like a fine story."

"Perhaps it is better that you rest now and enjoy the fine weather," she said, a bit of crimson crawling up her neck and cheeks.

"No, please read more of that."

Her finger traced the spot where she'd left off.

" 'And David sent messengers, and took her; and she came in unto him, and he lay with her; for she was purified from her uncleanness: and she returned unto her house.' "

She stopped again and turned her face away, and I knew she was embarrassed reading such things to a man.

"I think I shall read to you another time," she said.

"It's OK, Sister," I said. "That's some fine

writing, whoever wrote it, and sounded even finer hearing you read it."

She stood and said: "I have to go now. I'll see you again later."

"Yes, ma'am," I said, and watched her hurry off. I felt damned bad about her embarrassment.

I was wearied from just the little effort to talk and listen. I closed my eyes there in the cooling shade of the big tree and listened to the bird singing its lonely song and knew what it was feeling, for I was feeling it, too.

I soon found myself walking in the land of the dead. My boy stood at the end of a long road, the light around him like a blaze of fire.

"Papa!" he called.

I tried to run to him but I couldn't get any closer. He just stood there calling for me. I came out of the dream like a man drowning.

The sky off to the east was a purple haze and the compound empty of everyone but me. I thought if I could I'd get up and start walking, but I couldn't.

Then the big man came lumbering toward me in the dying light and he eased his large frame down next to mine and said—"Here."—and extended his hand and in it were the makings of a cigarette already rolled. I took it with shaking fingers, and then he struck a match he'd pulled from somewhere I couldn't even see, and the match head flared into a flame and I lighted the shuck off it before he snapped it out. The light gleamed against his dark blue-black skin and jumped into his wet eyes before he snuffed it.

"How's that do you?" he said when I'd taken a draw that crawled down into my sore chest like a muskrat trying to chew its way out.

I coughed and held my fist against my breastbone.

"It tastes just like sweet sorrow," I said.

"I bet it does."

"You didn't bring some whiskey, too, did you?" I said.

He shook his head, the cotton hair soft white in the dying evening.

"A man would have to be some sort of prophet to find anything 'round here to drink stronger than coffee or water," he said. "He'd have to turn the water into wine he wanted a drink."

He smiled then and his teeth gleamed white in his dark face.

"I guess I amuse you," I said.

"Some," he said.

"Well, it's worth it for this here," I said, putting the cigarette to my lips and giving it another try, prepared this time for the deeper breath.

"Best get you back inside so they can feed you," he said.

"You live here?" I said.

"No," he said. "I live yonder." He pointed a thick finger. "Got a wife waiting on me ever' night

102

with supper on the table. Mostly fried chicken, chickpeas, mashed up potatoes, gravy, corn when it's available, squashes. Yum, yum."

"And I get some more turtle soup," I said.

He grinned all the more.

"It's good for you, I hear," he said.

"You like it?" I said.

He shook his head.

"I'd have to be pretty hard up to eat water had a turtle cooked up in it," he said.

"Yeah, me, too."

He helped me back inside and that night I supped on soup that had a turtle cooked up in it and thought about Lincoln Johnson eating fried chicken.

It didn't seem fair.

Chapter Fourteen

Sometime that next morning Lincoln Johnson stopped by my bed, looked at me with those wary, weary eyes.

"I told Bess about you," he said.

"Who's Bess?"

"My missus. I told her you was scrawny as that chicken she wrung the neck of and cooked up and how I thought you could stand a decent meal and she said . . . 'Do he like chicken?' And I said . . . 'Show me a man who don't.' And she said to bring you on home for supper if you're up for it and I told her I'd ask you. So, that's what I'm doing, asking . . . do you want to come to supper tonight?"

I'd had a rough night and was feeling the aftereffect, like my skin was raked over and my bones were trying to heal but wouldn't.

"I might not live till tonight," I said.

"I seen your kind before," he said. "Tough as old boot leather, tough as a rooster you can't catch nor kill with a hatchet. You'll make it."

"You know more than me, then."

"These folks here is good and generous, but truth is, they don't have much to give other than the time and care. Food here is poorly and too little of it. Turtle soup, ha! Who can live on turtle soup and bread and water?"

"To tell the truth that soup tastes like something they wash socks in," I said.

He looked around to see if anyone was listening. "You didn't hear that come outta my mouth."

"I don't know where my clothes are," I said.

"Remember I told you that you didn't have no clothes on when I found you."

"Well, I don't reckon it's proper I go to supper with no clothes on," I said.

He looked at me oddly.

"I got work out in front of me yet, but later on, when I get off, I'll come by and bring you some clothes, then take you on to my place. Bess will cook you up some good eating. Put some meat back on your bones."

"Why would you do such kindness like that to a stranger?"

His eyes stayed on me like a hunting dog pointing a bird in the bush.

"You mean why would I do such a kindness to a white man?"

"No. I mean a stranger . . . somebody you don't know anything about."

"You know what He say, don't you?"

"Who is he?"

Lincoln Johnson pointed toward the ceiling.

"Man upstairs?"

"You mean God?"

"I mean Jesus, yes."

"I'm not exactly any expert on that business," I said.

" 'What you do to the least of these you do to me.' That's what He say. I'm a Christian man, Mister Blood. You a Christian?"

"No, I'm not anything."

"Yes, you are. You just don't know yet what you are."

I watched the big man lumber down the aisle between the beds, the one he had most recently mopped and gleamed with the shadow of him. I saw him stopping here and there to take a chamber pot, pour a patient a glass of water, and so forth. I wondered what was the measure of a man to empty chamber pots and mop floors and care for the sick the way that Lincoln Johnson did it?

I shucked into a cotton robe provided for the primary purpose of having me not strut about naked—not that I was able to do much strutting, naked or otherwise—and went outside to sit in the sun. I still craved a drink of bourbon, but the craving was less so now.

Sitting there in the courtyard, I saw Sister Margaret push a wheelchair with a one-legged man in it. She said something to him after she'd parked him in the shade, then went back inside. I watched the man reach into his robe pocket and take out his makings. Well, nobody had any whiskey around that place, so I limped over.

"I sure could stand a smoke myself," I said casually. He was a young man with dark hair and a goatee. Handsome as an actor.

He looked me up and down, grinned, and handed over his pouch and papers.

"Help yourself," he said. His voice was soft as magnolia and deeply Southern.

"Thank you kindly," I said.

I fixed myself a shuck, then lighted it off the one the young man was smoking. Inhaling still hurt my chest to where it felt a little like my breast-bone was snapping like a dry twig.

"You ever smoke one of them things before?" the young man asked, watching me hold myself against the coughing.

"More'n than I probably should have," I said. "It just makes it a little harder when you've been shot through the middle. Made my lungs sore."

"That's what I heard about you," he said. "I sort of make it my business to know among whom I might be dying. You've heard it said, of course, that a man is known by the company he keeps." He smiled and smoked, carelessly, as though he had not a care in the world.

"I suppose you're like Vitter," he said.

"Never heard of him," I said.

"Oh, Vitter was a fellow came through here in the early spring. He'd been shot about like you were . . . several times through the body by a jealous husband. Vitter prided himself in regaling us all with stories about himself and the wives of other men. It was almost like a badge of courage to him to get shot. Well, like yourself, he'd been shot several times and he was actually getting better and probably would have walked out of here a whole man until that same husband caught him going to the privy and gave him one more lead pill. And like that . . . Vitter was killed."

The young man snapped his fingers, then fell silent for a time. Then, while he fixed himself another shuck, he began to talk again.

"I lost my leg sawing down a tree," he said. "I thought it would fall one way and it fell the other."

"Damn' poor luck."

"I should have just sawn my leg off and saved me the labor of that damned big oak taking it."

"Might have been the best way," I said, not wanting to sound disagreeable, but finding some humor in it, too.

"Doc says he knows of a man in Cheyenne will make me a new one out of wood. Wood! Wood took my leg and now I am fated to end up with wood for a leg. Damnedest thing, ain't it? I'd like it if they made me a wooden leg out of the tree I sawed down. Now that would be some justice, wouldn't it?"

"I knew a man had a peg leg once," I said, remembering Peg Leg Harry Lee who was a Mississippi riverboat captain.

"How'd he take to it, walking with a peg leg?"

"Seemed to take to it fine," I said.

He studied on that thought for a time, both of us there in the shade, smoking, looking at our futures.

"They got some good-looking women around here," the young man said then, exhaling streams of smoke through his nostrils. "Trouble is, they're all married to Jesus and won't a one of them consider a proposal from a real man. I might only have one leg, but at least I'm not dead. You'd think a woman would want a live one-legged man over a two-legged ghost, wouldn't you?"

The young man's lips curled into a smile at the thought.

"That's a hard one to compete with all right," I said.

"You wouldn't want Jesus after you for stealing His woman." The young man chortled. "I guess that would be about the damned biggest mistake a man could make."

"I don't know about that. I reckon if you believe in such things."

"I once had to jump out a second-story window in Omaha because this lady's husband came home early," the young man said. "You'd've thought it was Jesus coming through the front door, hollering . . . 'Ida, Ida Mae.' I was a real rascal back then."

I couldn't help but smile, too. The young man couldn't have been more than twenty-odd years old and talking about *back then,* as if he was fifty.

"I guess, if I have to do any more jumping out windows, it will have to be out the first floor window," the young man continued. "I don't see me climbing any stairs with a wood leg, or jumping, either. I better stick to widows and other single women from now on. Not these here." He waved a hand in the direction of the nuns, tending patients out in the courtyard.

"I'm sure Jesus would appreciate you not going after His wives," I said.

There was a thread of sadness in the young man's jokes.

The light dimmed in the sky.

Then soon enough Lincoln Johnson came around, handed me a blue shirt and a pair of faded jeans, socks, and a pair of old rough boots with brass eyelets.

"They just some old clothes I figured would fit you," he said. "Fellow who owned them was about your size."

"You sure he won't miss them?"

"He won't miss 'em. His name was Jim Vitter. He died some time ago. We keep the clothes of them who die for folks who don't. Keep their shoes, too."

I didn't say anything about knowing the ballad of Jim Vitter as I worked my way into his clothes, his shoes, but it felt in a way like maybe he was still looking for them—that the dead who go violently don't find peace. At least I heard that once from a woman in Little Rock.

"Dead man's clothes, huh?"

"Nobody'll know but me and you."

I dressed with the slowness of a hundred-year-old man, laced up the boots, and it winded me by the time I finished.

"Got a wagon outside," the orderly said.

We went outside slowly and the big man helped me climb up into a spring wagon hitched to a big bay mule.

"It ain't far where I live," he said, taking up the seat next to me.

Maybe a mile is all we traveled before turning off at his place. A dirt lane led to a small clapboard house that looked freshly whitewashed and was perched on the lip of a cutbank below which a stream of water curled and flowed away, vanishing around a bend. A large dark woman came to stand in the doorjamb lit by a setting sun, a red polka dot bandanna tied around her hair. Her largeness seemed to match the size of Lincoln Johnson.

"Ambrosia, this here is Mister Royce Blood, the one I told you about that likes fried chicken so well."

"Welcome to our home, Mister Blood."

"Thank you kindly."

There was an old scarred table set in the yard with blue chinaware, bowls of sweet potatoes, biscuits, cooked dandelions, a basket of fried chicken, a pot of coffee, and a pie with a cheese-cloth laid over it. The smell of home-cooked food nearly caused me to faint.

We sat down and they clasped hands with mine. Then Mr. Johnson invoked a prayer, which I pretended to say but merely mumbled my words.

I was surprised how hungry I was, but then it didn't take me long to realize afterward that I had overdone it. The food rebelled and I felt it trying to escape.

"I need to go to the privy," I said when the first wave of nausea hit.

I tried my best to muffle my retching, not wanting the woman to feel bad about her cooking.

111

It wasn't her cooking; it was I just wasn't ready for so much.

"God damn," I muttered, disgusted with myself, swiping at the spittle.

I returned to the house.

"Got coffee and pie for you," Ambrosia said sweetly, as if she did not know of my condition, or that I was a white man and pretty well godless. They were sweet people and I was grateful for their kindness.

I tried to nibble at the sweet potato pie and sip the coffee.

"It's the best food I ate since . . ." I started to say "since I was married and happy," but caught myself in time and fell silent. The bullets felt like they were still inside my chest, rattling around in my lungs.

"Best get you back to the infirmary or the sisters will think I stole you," Lincoln Johnson said. I could see the concern in his eyes.

We rode back in the half dark of a moon-filled night. The mule pulling the wagon didn't seem to need any guidance. It had walked this same road so many times it could walk it blind.

"Here, have you a taste of this," Lincoln said, handing me a pint bottle he pulled from back of the seat under some burlap sacks.

"I figured you for a teetotaler," I said, taking the bottle, pulling the cork, and letting the liquid fire spill down my throat.

"I keep it for snakebite," he said. "And you sure enough look snake bit to me."

I took another pull and handed it back to him, and watched him take a pull.

"You don't look so snake bit, Mister Johnson," I said.

He wiped his mouth with the back of his hand and said: "This is in case I is bit on the way home."

He halted the mule outside the infirmary wall and helped me down and through the gate.

"You be OK to get in by yourself?"

"Yes," I said. "Thank Ambrosia for me again."

"She already knows."

"I reckon so."

"Might I ask you somethin'?"

"You've a right."

"Why'd somebody want to shoot you so bad?"

"I don't know."

"Reckon maybe you should figure it out?"

"That is my aim."

"I figure if whoever it was shot you finds out you ain't killed, well, they might come 'round, trying to do it again."

"I've thought of that."

"Well, good night, Mister Blood."

"Good night, Mister Johnson."

I leaned against the gate until Lincoln Johnson had driven off, then retched again. The whiskey did not sit well with me, either, for the first time.

Maybe it was a sign I didn't need it any more. If something doesn't want to stay with you, why should you stay with it?

I went inside and removed my clothes and stretched out on the nice clean bed and listened to other men groaning and snoring and smelled their sickness, and I knew I had to get out of that place soon.

Lincoln Johnson was right about whoever it was who shot me. I could wait for him to come find me—like the fellow who found that Vitter fellow—or I could go in search of the shooter and get him first.

Getting him before he got me seemed like the smart play.

Should have killed me, I thought. *Should have killed me.*

Chapter Fifteen

More days came and went as I knitted myself together—the wounds going from painful to itching to downright bothersome to forgetting they were there.

My mind was on the man who had shot me and what had happened to Sara. I grew determined to find out.

The summer season brought afternoon storms. The day would start out bright and clear and by early afternoon columns of white clouds would form over the mountains, turn slowly gray, then lower themselves over the land and spill rain before leaving again. The air would always be washed clean, but those storms didn't do a thing to clean my mind.

Sister Margaret would often offer to read to me, but it was always something safe, about God's love and redemption, and never again did she read anything to me from the darker parts of the Good Book.

I was watching a growing storm with lightning shaking through its mass as it approached the infirmary. The good sister was reading to me, but I was only half listening.

"Ask you something?" I said.

She lifted her gaze from the page.

"What made you choose this life?"

A soft smile played at the edges of her mouth.

"What makes any of us choose whatever life we choose?"

"Good question," I said. "I couldn't say. I reckon some of it has to do with circumstances . . . where we were born and who to . . . things like that."

"Or, maybe," she said, "God has a plan for each of us."

"Then I sure wish he'd let me in on it, because it sure seems like a pretty lousy plan to me so far."

She lowered her eyes to the Bible again, then lifted them back to me.

"God says our highest glory is to serve Him and in serving Him we serve others."

"It's a long way from where I'm at," I said. "You ever have a beau?"

She smiled shyly.

"Yes, I did once."

"And you chose this life over one with him?"

"He died. And with him, my romantic heart."

"I know all about that," I said.

"Sometimes I think the living have it worse than the dead. We're left with the hungering heartbreak and they are in heaven, at peace. Do you believe in heaven, Mister Blood?"

"I can't say I believe in any of it, Sister."

"It's all a matter of faith."

"I know it is, but I only ever had that sort of faith in myself . . . and look where that got me. Hard to believe in anything I can't see."

"Perhaps some day you will find a reason to believe in Jesus Christ."

"Read me some more, if you will."

And so she did, reading from the book of Ecclesiastes. Her soft voice, soothing as a cool drink to a thirsting tongue, or maybe the words were quenching my thirsting heart.

I dozed and awoke to a thunderclap. Sister Margaret was no longer sitting there.

The first raindrops splattered on the stones of

the courtyard's paths, large and dark and round. Lincoln Johnson came and asked if I needed help getting inside. I told him no and rose stiffly, feeling the storm as much inside my bones as outside.

"I need a favor," I said as we ducked in out of the rain.

"What would that be, Mister Blood?"

"I need you to carry me into the nearest town."

"In this rain?"

"No, after the rain stops."

"You need something from there, I can just get it for you next time."

"Just need to get there is all."

"It's a bad place to get to."

"I reckon it is, considering how I was greeted last time I went."

"Yes, suh."

Sister Margaret came into the darkened room later when the storm was in full force outside. You could hear the big raindrops pinging against the metal roof, hear them boiling up on the ground.

"Lincoln told me you want him to take you to Two Cents," she said.

"That's right. I think I've taken up enough of your time and some good bed space another will need more than me."

"Is that really why you're going?" she said.

"I need to find somebody, Sister."

"The man who shot you?"

"Yes, but first I need to find a woman."

She looked skeptical.

"I don't mean in the way it sounds," I said. "She was with me when I got shot and I think maybe she got shot, too."

She shook her head.

"Whatever is your business is your business, Mister Blood. There's no need to explain. But if you mean to take a life, then I'd pray that you'd reconsider."

"You might do better saving your prayers for those who are going to want them, Sister."

"God says we should forgive those who transgress against us."

"I never read the Book, ma'am. If I'm to be judged, then let me be judged, but I know what I have to do and I aim to do it."

Fret lined her kind features.

The crack of thunder rattled the earth beneath our feet. If it was God's doing, there wasn't anything a puny man like me was going to do to go against Him. But I wasn't trying to go against Him; I just wanted to bring a little justice to those just as puny as me.

"We can give you a little money to help you on your way," Sister Margaret said.

"Not necessary."

"What do you plan to live on, locusts and honey like John the Baptist in the wilderness?"

"I've lived on less."

"That I don't doubt, Mister Blood."

Another thunderclap caused her to start. I was a little jumpy myself.

"Lie back and let me check your bandages before you go," she said.

Her hands were tender, the fingers cool, ministering.

"This one is still leaking a bit," she said.

"Plug it if you can."

"You could still get an infection, something very serious."

"I could die of old age, sitting around here."

"You're a restless man, aren't you, Mister Blood?"

"Yes. Always was."

"Quick to go and get yourself shot again."

"Perhaps. But this time I plan on doing some shooting back."

"May I ask if you were shot because of this woman you must go and find?"

"I can't say why I was shot . . . maybe, but I doubt it. I think it was more likely the man I was looking for who robbed the stage and killed my friend. He didn't want me to find him, so he found me first."

"The world you live in sounds dangerous."

"Not till most recent. After my wife and boy died, I crawled down in the bottom of a bottle and life wasn't so bad down there. I did not trouble anybody and nobody troubled me. I didn't ask for this, Sister, but now that it has come to visit me, I won't turn away from it, either."

She finished changing my stained bandage. The puckered wounds were brown and scabbed over and I didn't even like looking at them because it made me angry every time I did.

"I . . . ," she started to say, then stopped and turned away. I watched her go down the hall. Rain hammered overhead like boys with tiny hammers.

First thing I need is a gun, I thought. I had already picked out one in my mind.

Lincoln came in the late afternoon. The storm had passed on to the east. He set his tired eyes upon me like a frustrated father trying to teach his son a lesson but failing to do so.

"You ready?"

"Been ready."

"I guess we can go then."

I sat up, and, when I bent to tie those donated boots, it felt like something heavy and sharp shifted inside my chest. I had to grit my teeth against the pain in order to stand.

"Let's go," I said, sucking in air. But before we could get to Lincoln's wagon outside the wall, Sister Margaret intervened.

"Here," she said, handing me an envelope.

"What's this?"

"Just a little something to sustain you until you can find your way."

Inside the envelope there was money and a rosary.

"I'm not Catholic," I said, holding the rosary in one hand.

"It doesn't matter if you believe you've found God or not. He has found you."

"I don't mean to sound ungrateful," I said. "But this won't help me none."

"It won't hurt you none, either, Mister Blood," she said in a teasing way, mocking my pattern of speech.

She pressed my fingers around the envelope.

"I'll pay you back the money soon as I'm able," I said.

"It's not necessary. Perhaps you'll come across another luckless and troubled soul someday you can help, and that will be payment enough."

"That how you see me, as a luckless and troubled soul?"

"You're spirit surely is."

I saw her for the first time not so much as the bride of Christ, but as a woman, gracious and lovely—the kind of woman any man could fall in love with—like my Ophelia.

"Thank you," I said.

"Go with God."

God probably would not want to go where I aim to go, I thought.

I got up into the wagon with some effort and took my place next to Lincoln Johnson. The air was still damp and heavy from the storm and the road was muddy, and Lincoln drove slowly so as not to weary his old mule.

"What you goin' do when you get there . . . you not knowing who it was shot you?"

"Get a gun, first thing."

"Might not even get that far if whoever it was sees you up and walking on the earth."

"Might not."

"A smart man would go the other way . . . away from that place.

"A smart man probably would."

"You don't seem like no fool."

"I never was that smart when it came to certain things."

Lincoln smiled, his teeth white as snow in a pile of coal. *How does a man get such good teeth?*

"They named that town wrong," he said. "Should've named it Not A Dime's Worth, for that's all it is."

"Maybe by the time I'm finished they'll change the name."

"You intendin' on makin' some changes?"

"Just a few."

"You're only one man, in case you ain't noticed? And a half shot-up one at that."

"Worst kind of man is one who don't think he's got anything more to lose, Mister Johnson."

"That how you feel . . . like you got nothin' more to lose?"

"Pretty much."

"I'll let you off at the place they sell guns. How will that be?"

"That will be aces."

"All right then."

And, as promised, he stopped his wagon in front of a small narrow store cobbled between a saloon and a barbershop with the words *GUNS BOUGHT AND SOLD* painted in crude lettering over the door.

"Well, sir, here you is."

"Thanks kindly for everything."

"I wish you luck with your business."

"I'll need it."

Before we shook hands, Lincoln reached behind the wagon seat and shook free a denim jacket with brass buttons.

"Thought you might want this old coat of mine. I sorta outgrowed it."

I felt embarrassed to take a man's coat, but I took it anyway in the spirit in which it was offered. There was a quiet strength in Lincoln Johnson's hand. Strength that had been there all that man's life, I suspected. A man's strength that was formed from hard labor and hard times he'd refused to let defeat him. It was a hand that had probably wrestled the devil and won, and rubbed away a child's tear.

"Tell your missus thanks again for that fine meal," I said.

The big man nodded, then turned his wagon around in the middle of the wide street, and started back in the direction we'd just come from.

I stepped inside the gun shop.

Chapter Sixteen

The man behind the gun counter had an evil scar that looked like someone had sliced his cheek ear to lip and someone else had done a bad job of sewing it up. He wore smoke-colored spectacles and was inlaying a wood stock of maple with a fine little metal tool.

He looked up when the bell above the door rang and stopped his work. He wore a greasy leather apron and the place smelled of gun oil and metal filings. There was a rack of various types of long guns along one wall—rifles and shotguns and sporting guns and even an old Civil War musket with a stock held together by a strand of wire.

"What can I do for you?" he said. His neck was grizzled with unshaven bristles that flashed like small silver needles.

"I want to buy a gun."

"That's why most come in here," he said. "What kind of gun? Handgun or long gun?"

"Shotgun," I said.

He rose up.

"Got several, anything in particular?"

I walked over to the rack. There, plain as any-thing, was my gun—the one Burt had given me that bad day I'd decided to try my hand at honest work.

"This one," I said. "How much?"

"Fifteen dollars and I'll throw in a box of shells."

"Fifteen, hell," I said, and turned to look at him. He'd stiffened considerable.

"That's my gun," I said.

He shook his head.

"Well, ain't you the prize," he said. "I don't see how that could be your gun when it's in my rack."

"Who gave you this?" I said.

"Nobody gave me nothing. I bought that gun."

"Who'd you buy it from?"

"What the hell business is that of yours?"

I crossed the room in three strides and, without saying a word, punched him just below that scar. I felt bone give way under the ruined flesh and he went down hard and I grabbed the half-carved maple wood stock and said: "If you want, I can beat you to death with this. Or, you can just answer my damned question."

His eye was already closing from the busted cheek bone and I would like to say I felt bad that I hit him but seeing my stolen gun standing in his rack, knowing that whoever shot me had taken it, and then sold it—well, I wasn't sorry for anything.

He looked up, holding one rough hand to his face.

"A woman sold it to me."

"What'd she look like?"

He described Belle Moon right down to her cold blue eyes.

I dug $2 out of the envelop and tossed it on the counter and said—"Get me a box of shells for my gun"—and turned and yanked it free of the rack and came back over and waited for him to get me a box of shells, then broke the breech and put one shell in each chamber and snapped it closed again.

He looked forlorn.

"See that," I said, pointing to what looked like some rust spots on the top of the twin barrels. "That's my god-damned blood."

I walked out with the box of shells in my pocket except for the pair that were in the shotgun.

I asked after the local law and was told how to find him.

His name was John Dove and he kept court at a place called the Hair of the Dog—a nasty little booze parlor down at the end of the main drag.

I found John Dove sitting with three others, playing some sort of cards—whist maybe—and I said: "I understand you're the law."

He looked up at me with a pair of porcine eyes like you might see on a blue shoat looking for its slops.

"What if I am?" he said.

"My name's Royce Blood," I said. "And I was shot in that hotel up the street. About three or four weeks ago."

The others playing cards with John Dove watched me like I was a rabbit and they were hunting pups —not quite sure what to do with me, if anything.

"Well, seems I heard about that," he said. "I was gone that week, fishing."

"So I was told."

"I like to fish," he said.

"When there's trouble afoot or otherwise," I said.

His piggish gaze fell to the shotgun in my grip.

He ordered a round of drinks for himself and his friends, and, when they came, he held his for a moment to his lips, looking at me over the top of his glass, then tossed it back. He was fat like a shoat hog, too, and had rust-colored gunfighter moustaches and I don't doubt that somewhere in his history he'd killed more than one man.

"What you want, mister?" he said, wiping his mouth with two fingers.

"I want to know where Gypsy Davy and Belle Moon are," I said.

"Gypsy Davy?" he hooted. "Belle Moon?"

The others seemed to be swallowing their grins.

I stepped back away from the table.

"I came here looking for them," I said. "But I also came looking for the woman who was with me that night. Tell me what happened to her."

He looked serious then, like a big fat rattler coiling in order to strike.

"There was a woman killed, yes," he said. "Just like I heard you was, so who the hell knows who is dead and who isn't?"

He looked about at his pals, and they smiled like they were all playing to an inside straight up against a pair of deuces.

"This is getting to be just like Jerusalem with all these dead people risen up and walking around," John Dove continued. I guess he thought he was being clever. He did not understand how close he was to being dead.

"Where would they have taken her if she was dead?" I said.

"The graveyard, I suspect. Ain't that usually where you take dead people?"

I looked at the others. They were close to walking in the light, too, as far as I was concerned. I had enough buckshot for all of them.

I'd seen a sign for an undertaker on the way to the saloon. Every town had one—it was the one constant business a man who didn't mind working in that line could count on.

"You've been real friendly," I said. "I also had a horse and wagon. Where might they have gone?"

He shrugged.

"I guess the way of all things," he said, and sniggered.

"I find Davy in this town I'm going to kill him," I said. "Just so you know."

The snigger went away.

"Nobody gets killed in my town 'less I do it," he said.

"You want to start now?" I said.

I'd learned over a lifetime of watching other men who will fight and who will try and talk you to death. The ones that will fight get right to it most generally. The fat man eased whatever was in his flesh and bone and let it settle back into that bloated body of his.

"I'll decide when the killing starts," he said.

"Good, just let me know."

I backed out, not trusting the son-of-a-bitch not to back shoot me. I know some talk about a code of honor and some have it, but most don't when it comes to being especially scared of the other man.

I hustled up to the undertaker's and found him nearly passed out drunk on a horsehair sofa inside. He tried to right himself at my entrance but struggled to do so.

"Do ya need a funeral?" he said in a slurred Irish accent. He was a little bitty fellow and his trousers were too short, showing off a pair of shiny shin bones. "For ya certainly don't look dead to me!" He laughed at his own joke. Always a bad sign of character.

I asked about Sara.

He shook his head.

"Last woman I buried was Maude Smith," he said. "I buried all three of her husbands before her, too. Got the whole family. Always do, always will."

"If a woman was to die in this town, wouldn't it be you who'd know about it?"

"I would," he said.

"So no young woman died, most specifically shot in that hotel across the street?"

He tried sitting up again, but fell back.

" 'Tis liquor that knows my name," he said, and shook his head. "Sorry, friend, I have not handled or otherwise disposed of any female flesh younger than old Maude who was nearly a hundred and looked every day of it, too." He wrinkled his nose at the thought, then added: "Nor have I touched any live female flesh that young in ages." He grinned, and closed his eyes.

I went out and across to the hotel, hoping to find the clerk that was on duty. But it wasn't the same man. The other one had black hair and this one was nearly bald and a lot older. I told him why I'd come.

"That would have been Purvis," he said.

"Where might I find him?"

"I heard he went to Omaha to become a carpenter," he said.

"How much you know about folks around these parts?" I said.

He shrugged.

"Don't know nothing."

I took the last of the money from the envelope and set it on the desk.

"It's yours if you can tell me where to find either Gypsy Davy or Belle Moon," I said.

He stared at it a long time.

"I don't nothing about a Gypsy Davy," he said, his fingers sort of dancing toward the money. "But I know Belle's got a ma or aunt or something living out west of here."

I had him tell me how to find her place, and then watched as he scooped the money up.

"You tell anybody I said anything about this," he said, "I'll deny it."

"Judas got thirty pieces of silver," I said. "You got nineteen dollars."

I walked down to the livery to see if I could find my horse and wagon. A Negro was pitching hay into the corral from a stack alongside the shed. A little dark-skinned girl sat on a wood bench, watching him.

I told him the situation. He just looked long at me. Then he said: "I heard about you."

"What'd you hear?" I said.

"Heard they killed you at the hotel. Some lady, too."

"You hear who it was killed me?" I said.

He shook his head. He had a horseshoe of graying hair and the top of his head gleamed with sun and sweat. He glanced over at the child.

"No," he said. "I din't hear no more than they was a killing."

"What about that horse and wagon?" I said.

He looked toward the barn.

"Tell you what," I said. "Saddle me the horse and you can keep the wagon."

I saw that he was studying on it. Then he nodded.

As he tightened the cinch on what used to be my horse, sort of, I said: "You hear of a Missus Moon who lives west of here?"

"They's a crazy old woman named that, yas."

I asked him to give me directions and he did. I forked the bay and gave the child a glance. Her eyes were large and white and dark in the centers. She was skinny and dressed raggedly but had the face of an angel.

I rode west until I spotted the low-lying shack.

There, sitting out front on an upturned wood keg, was Dew Hardy, looking like a man who'd gone to a razor fight without his razor.

Chapter Seventeen

The Pinkerton was peeling an apple with a small paring knife. He stopped peeling when I rode up. His face was lashed with red stripes and his nose was a lot more crooked than I remembered it and his right eye looked a little off.

"I see you made it," he said.

"I come looking for Belle's ma or aunt or whatever the hell she is," I said. "What are you doing here?"

"Surviving mostly," he said, then peeled some more of the apple, letting the long string of red skin curl off the blade of his knife like a snake's skin.

His hair hung wetly down over his face when he dipped his head to study the apple he peeled. His clothes were poor but clean. He wore an old pair of brogan shoes that looked like they chaffed his ankles; you could see because his pants were high-water.

He looked up again and bit into the soft white pulp and looked pleased at its taste.

Then the front door of the shack opened and a woman stepped out, carrying a long-barreled gun that was as tall as she was—an old ball-and-powder. She was bony as a yard chicken with a yard chicken's beak for a nose and the same beady eyes a yard chicken has, and she said: "What you want, mister?"

"Etta Winesop, Belle's aunty," Dew Hardy said, thumbing back over his shoulder. "You best be careful, she's mighty protective."

"Put that gun away, ma'am, before you kill somebody," I said.

"That's what I aim to do if you've come to take him!" she said.

I looked at the Pinkerton. He looked sheepish as hell.

"I didn't come to take him," I said. "I come to find out where Belle Moon is."

"I don't know no such body," she said. Her voice was pinched like a woman who is always fearful.

"You keep waving that gun around, I'm going to have to take it off you," I said.

"Just you damn' well try, mister."

"She's a pickle," Dew Hardy said, eating more of his apple.

She had ringlets of ash gray hair and no beauty to her whatsoever. If you'd have wanted a spell cast on you, she might have been the one to see.

"Go on, git!" she said to me.

"No," I said. "I'm not gitting anywhere until you tell me what I came here for."

She advanced and stood next to Dew Hardy.

"Run him off," she said to the Pinkerton.

"With what, Etta, this here paring knife?"

"Take my gun and shoot him."

"What would I do with him if I was to do that?"

"Bury him out back."

"Now, Etta, I know this fellow and he's not so bad."

"You going off with him?"

"I wasn't planning on it," Dew Hardy said. He bit another chunk of the apple and chewed it thoughtfully, then added: "But then, I wasn't planning on a lot of things."

"I saved your worthless hide," she said.

"That you most certainly did and for it I am eternally grateful."

"I want to know where Belle Moon is even if I have to do bad things to you," I threatened.

She punched Dew Hardy in the shoulder with the butt of her gun.

"Defend me!" she cried.

Dew Hardy hummed and kept eating his apple as though she wasn't there.

"You worthless bastard!" she said, and stalked into the house.

"What's between you two?" I said.

"I owe her," Dew Hardy said.

"How the hell did you end up here?" I said.

He bit off the last piece of apple, then tossed the core aside.

"I was hot on their trail," he said, gazing off to nowhere in particular—just the great beyond. "I thought I had run them to ground, too."

I looked toward the house to make sure the old crone wasn't planning on assassinating me from a window.

"Anyway, I tracked them down to where I found Belle." He paused as though troubled by the memory and shook his head slowly. "You want to know how I found her?"

"Go on with it," I said, growing impatient.

"Naked, is how. Sitting on her horse without a stitch on . . . under the shade of a buckeye tree. I seen that and I fell for the oldest trick in the book."

"She led you into an ambush," I said.

Again he shook his head.

"I never seen a woman that beautiful, naked or otherwise," he said. "It dazzled my thinking. You know I'm like every other man . . . led by my pecker and it ain't got no sense."

"Davy was waylaying for you and Belle led you to him."

"I was the rabbit and him the fox," the Pinkerton said. "Trapped me easy as anything."

"Surprised he didn't kill you," I said.

Dew Hardy looked up with a half-satisfied look.

"He sure gave it all he had," he said. "He trussed me to a fence post with barb wire, then used his fists on me, then he whipped me with his belt so the blood would draw flies and ants to me. Belle just sat there, enjoying the show. Coldest bitch I ever encountered in my life."

I heard the old woman howling inside the shack.

"She's just grieving," Dew Hardy said.

"Grieving for what?" I said.

"She's certain you're going to take me away from her."

"Does she think she owns you?"

"She does," he said. "Told me that she saved my life and that I was forever hers. Who was I to argue? She came along just hours before I would have perished. All eaten up by flies and ants and mosquitoes. I could hear wolves howling in the dark. They smelled my blood and would have eaten the meat off my bones. I was tied up for three days and nights before she came along and found me. She took to me like a cat to sweet milk." Dew Hardy looked pleased with himself in an odd sort of way.

"All well and good," I said, "but what I don't understand is why you haven't gotten her to tell you where Davy and Belle are and tracked them down . . . you wanted that damned stolen gold so bad."

He squinted. A twitch started under his off eye.

"Tell you the truth," he said, "I'm not sure I'd want to catch them after the way they did me. The second night out there, tied to that fence post, I talked to Jesus and the devil. They both came to visit me, and they was arguing over which one should take my soul and I was arguing I wasn't yet ready to go nowheres." A tear leaked from his eye.

"They scared you bad, huh?" I said.

He nodded.

"You know Davy shot me back in that hotel," I said.

He nodded again.

"I know," he said. "I was the one who found you bleeding and hardly alive. I was the one who carried you out to that infirmary and dropped you off."

"What of the woman, Sara?" I said.

He shook his head slowly.

"I couldn't do nothing but bury her. She lived only for a little while . . . dead by the time I got you to the infirmary."

"Why the kindness?" I said.

"Hell if I know," he said. "And that's the truth."

It didn't tote—for a man to do another a kindness like that—but then Dew Hardy was a strange son-of-a-bitch if there ever was one.

The old crone inside the shack screamed like she was being murdered.

"She goes out of her head sometimes," Dew Hardy said.

"I'm not leaving here until she tells me where Belle and Davy are," I said.

The Pinkerton stood slowly—like an old man too long in cold water.

"I've sort of taken to her," he said, looking toward the shack. "Given the circumstances and all."

"Do what you have to," I said.

He nodded.

"There's love and then there's gold," he said. "Tell you how it's going to be. You promise to let me keep whatever gold we get off Davy and Belle, and I'll go ask Etta where they are at."

I thought on it for a minute. I could kill him, of

course, or at least shoot him up pretty good, but what would be the point? I could burn the place, but there was no guarantee she'd tell me anything. I either wanted to return that gold to Deadwood or find Davy and kill him.

"Go on then," I said. "Ask her."

"It might take a little bit . . . you willing to wait?"

"Hell," I said, looking up at the sun.

He went into the house and I waited.

An hour passed and he came out again, hitching up his pants and looking like he'd been in a tussle of some magnitude. Three or four times while he was inside I heard the old woman screaming and I had to close my eyes at the thought of what Dew Hardy might be doing to her. But it didn't sound like screams of a woman in distress as much as one having a hell of a good time.

"You get it out of her?" I said as he walked over to a piebald mule and took an old saddle and saddled it.

"I got it in her and out of her," he said with a grin.

"Jesus, I don't need to know the details," I said.

He smacked his lips as he tightened the cinch. I noticed the wood grips of a small handgun sticking out of the right front pocket of his jeans.

"They're in Cheyenne," he said.

I looked toward the house.

"You kill her?" I said.

"No. Fact is, she probably ain't never felt so good."

He forked the saddle and the horse's ears pricked up.

"We'll go back to Two Cents," he said. "And catch the train to Cheyenne."

"What about your lady friend?" I said.

"Oh," he said, "I imagine she'll work loose from them knots I tied in an hour or two."

"Knots?" I said.

"Not to worry," he said. "She prefers it that way."

We rode clip-clop back to Two Cents and I couldn't get the picture out of my mind of that old woman tied up and . . .

Chapter Eighteen

Gypsy Davy said: "I got the girl and I got the gold and what more can a man possibly want except to see the shining face of Jesus when he dies? Oh, but you are a pert thing, gal. Pert as I ever seen. And the way you handled that *pistola*, well, a thing of beauty, it truly was."

Belle Moon was in her bloomers, bare from the waist up in the fancy hotel room she and Davy had rented in Cheyenne, a long way from Two Cents—that dung heap. It had been almost two months since they robbed the Deadwood stage, shot the place all to hell, and left the dead in their

140

wake—including a few of their own: Boss Walker and his boy, Bill, Charley Evans, and Frank Skin.

"Oh, those were some lusty boys," she said, "Boss and them."

"Danged right. Kept them hungry for the sins of life . . . lead them along like pigs to the slaughter. They never seen it come, Belle, did they?"

"Poor Frank," Belle said. "That stranger blew off his arm and I guess we killed him out of kindness and done him a good turn, for he surely would have bled out slow and painfully."

"Yes, we done Frank a good turn and that's how we must look at it. Them other boys, too. If we hadn't assassinated them, they'd sooner or later all end up in prison. We done them good turns, too."

"We did it right, Davy. We were merciful in tendering them to the grave," she said, staring out at the rain drizzling down from a shrouded sky, like some old widow gone to weep at the grave of her lover. Tears falling over her ashen cheeks is the way Belle thought of it—the rain.

"They were led by their peckers instead of their brains," she added with a cheery smile whilst holding a glass of the champagne ordered to their room. $10 a bottle and worth every sip. "Such is the curse of men . . . to be led by their peckers instead of their brains."

"Does that include present company?" Davy said.

"Present company excluded, love."

He smiled from the bed upon which he reclined, sunk into the comfort of a feather mattress, his head and long hair resting upon a blue silk pillow. He was modest in proportion, a figure nearly as slight as she in size, a somewhat sensual face and mouth, though hidden by his dark moustaches. He'd recently shaved his beard. It had itched too much with lice.

"I am normally a woman who enjoys a good cocktail, but this champagne will do just fine," Belle said.

Gypsy Davy's stark nakedness compared to the pale of a fish's belly. He kept his guns nearby, the way he preferred his guns to be.

"When I pulled you out of that stink hole in Deadwood, you were lucky to drink watered-down booze with them crusty miners and gut-starved cowpokes . . . and look at you now, a real, genuine lady."

Belle did not care much to be reminded of their beginnings.

"Ha! I was a lady long before you were ever a gentleman."

"I was never a gentleman, but a two-gun killer all the way. My pappy gave me a pistol the day I was born and taught me to shoot it the day after. Now get your pretty tail on over to this bed and let's have another go around, you and me, because you know ol' Davy is glory bound. And if you want to ride along, you best hop this train." His grin said it all.

Belle drained the contents of her glass down her gullet and jumped on the bed where the two tangled not once but thrice before they fall apart like an egg cracked open and panting like thirsty dogs.

"What I want to know is," she said, "what happens when the money is all spent and the time comes to get more . . . you without a gang?"

"Thieves and would-be thieves are a dime a dozen," Davy said. "I'll just put together a new bunch."

"Got anyone in particular in mind?"

"I was thinking most recent of Blackbird and Little Dick Longwinter . . . neither too bright, but both as hard as swallowing a can of rusty nails."

"Little Dick Longwinter!" she shouted with glee. "Is that his name for real?"

"So he calls himself," Davy said.

"Well, it surely would be a long winter if his first name is true."

"You're quite the wit, you are, Belle."

"Ain't I, though. You know it's quite rare to have both beauty and brains in a woman, don't you?"

"I got a good eye for horses and women," Davy said. "How about some more of that bubbly juice?"

"The champagne's clear across the room chilling in a bucket of ice."

"So?"

"I hope you ain't planning on me becoming your personal slave."

"No, just my woman . . . and a woman is to serve her man."

"Well, maybe for now I am your woman," Belle said.

"For evermore."

She rose from the bed and sashayed across the room in a deliberate fashion so he could watch the wiggle of her buttocks, full and round and just right for a man of his nature. She was once the best white whore in all of Deadwood Gulch according to those who knew such facts. And once Davy had heard her name upon the lips of so many men, he just had to find out for himself. And by God, it was true. He never in all his rambling glory days met a woman who could do it like Belle Moon could, or had such a bloodlust in her.

"How you feel about robbing and killing?" he'd asked that first night of their romance.

"Same as I do about riding horses and screwing handsome men like yourself," she'd replied.

So he let her in on the plan he had to knock over the Deadwood stage, told her about his gang—Boss and Bill Walker, Charlie Evans and Frank Skin. She did not say it aloud, but knew three-fourths of those boys intimately already in her professional dealings. Boss and his boy Bill were a combo act who never did anything separately, including their whoring. It was fine by her—double team, double pay. Charlie Evans just liked to talk mostly because he wasn't sure what he was all about on the inside and uncertain with women in general. As far as Belle was concerned, getting paid to listen was a lot easier than getting rode like a pony for the express mail.

"Why do you come to me if you don't know if you like women or not?" she'd asked Charlie that first time when he admitted he didn't know if he could fornicate with her.

"I'm trying to prove to myself it's not just something in my head that makes me think otherwise," he said.

"Your way of thinking is as confusing as a Chinese puzzle," she said.

"I mean it ain't that I don't like women . . . I just ain't sure, and feel all strange around them. Of course I'm relying on you to keep this private between us."

"Are you trying to say you like your own kind better than a gal?"

"I ain't trying to say nothing."

Well, Charlie gave it his best effort, but his best proved not too good. So he'd pay her to tell the other boys waiting downstairs, waiting for him to return to regale them with tales of his sexual prowess. Charlie's money was as solid as any other man's even if his pecker was not. So it didn't matter a wit to her one way or the other. The only fellow of Gypsy's now assassinated gang that she had not known was the cross-eyed devil, Frank Skin, who, when it came time to put a bullet in him, she gladly did. For, knowing Frank Skin a little, was to know him a lot.

He had had bad breath and rotted teeth and fingers yellow from cigarette smoking and never had a kind thing to say to her. And once, when they were out of earshot of Davy, he'd whispered hotly: "I'd like to screw you with a gin bottle." She'd been around enough men to know some were born cruel and stayed that way all their lives. Frank Skin was such a man, clear up to the day she shot him out on the road and watched his head explode like a fat plum bashed by a sledge. It was akin to sexual pleasure to put a bullet into that mean son-of-a-bitch.

"We'll leave us a trail of blood," Davy had said that day on the road. "From sea to shining sea. . . ."

Davy often mused and waxed poetic when he was drunk and happy. He kept a banjo he liked to strum, and his voice was high-pitched and nasal when he sang. He had no true musical talent except what he fantasized. But none of this lacking deterred him from trying. He further enjoyed writing ballads, and had been working on one about him and Belle since they first started their life of crime together.

Davy and Belle, the Satans from hell
Ride wild horses on the outlaw trail.
They sing and they dance & their guns
Are ablaze just like their romance

Doggerel, of course. It was as far as he'd gotten before becoming stumped, but he was as nearly proud of it as he was of the carnage and mayhem the two had created.

"Life is but a short sweet season in the eons of time itself," he said to Belle as he drank straight from the bottle of champagne. She rolled her eyes.

"You should have been a play actor," she said. "You'd 'a' made a dandy one."

The take of the strongbox came to just over $10,000 and they had spent it generously, having journeyed by train to San Francisco, then up to Alaska by steamer where they saw bears ten feet tall and mountains that looked painted against the sky. Davy bought Belle a cross made from the penis bone of a whale, saying, as he tied it around her neck: "Sort of fits you perfect, the whole notion, don't it?"

They had lived like a king and queen while in San Francisco, but the police there in that town were good at what they did, and what they did best was catch outlaws, thieves, bunko artists, shysters, counterfeiters, and every other sort of con and criminal activity.

"We need to be on our best behavior around here," Davy had warned.

"I agree," Bell had said.

So they pretended to be rich swells from back East and took a suite of rooms at the Palace Hotel on Market Street and ate oysters and lobsters and three-inch-thick steaks in the dining room and washed down pickled elk hearts with good Kentucky bourbon and smoked dollar cigars. Belle's beauty drew the attention of all the other swells in the place, much to Gypsy's pleasure, for he enjoyed having other men take notice of Belle and encouraged her to be flirtatious, thinking, as he did, it might lead to some scheme they could pull later on—luring some rich gent up to the room, then at very moment the pair were in *flagrante delicto*, Gypsy would burst into the room with his gun in hand declaring the gent had seduced Gypsy's wife—one Belle Moon—and demand some form of recompense or else!

Gypsy told Belle about his plan.

"That seems so desperate," she said. "And besides, the police will find us out quick and clap us in jail. They're not like those two-bit stars in the Dakotas."

"I'm only saying if we should find ourselves in a pinch . . . before I can put a new gang together and go rob the bank here in town . . . the one that sits on the corner . . . that big one made of stone with the big winders."

"Bank! What do you know about robbing banks?" Belle declared.

He nodded with mirth when he told her if Frank and Jesse James could rob banks with aplomb, so could he.

"Jesse's dead and Frank's on the lam," she reminded him.

"That means there is more opportunity for us then, don't it?" Davy said.

At the time, they had been eating oysters and washing them down with champagne at the Inter-Ocean and Belle nearly choked on a pearl, spat it out, and held it to the light and said: "Look what I found."

"You see," Davy said. "Luck is with us every step of the way."

"Well, if anybody could make Frank and Jesse look like pikers, it would be you, Davy," Belle said still in wonderment at having found a pearl.

Davy grinned and kissed her cheek.

"You are one handsome devil," she said.

He winked and replied: "Don't I know it."

"I've something to confess," she said, giddy with life. "I was once a married woman."

"I ain't surprised."

"How many other men's wives have you known?"

"Not nearly enough," he said with his boyish grin. She believed she had never seen a man as pretty as Gypsy Davy. "When and where was you married, Belle?"

"I had a husband back in Kansas," she said. "I was young and too naïve to know better than to hitch my star to one man."

"He must have been something to capture a wildcat like you."

"He was a sodbuster."

"You . . . married to a sodbuster? I don't believe it."

"It's true. I was just seventeen at the time and innocent as baby Jesus."

"Still, I don't believe it. I doubt you were ever so innocent, Belle."

"Well, I was once."

"What happened to him?"

"He got dead."

"Do tell. . . ."

"Somebody stuck a knife in him."

"How utterly fascinating. Do you know who it was did the deed?"

"It was me. I caught him cheating on me with a neighbor's daughter . . . a mere child of thirteen. A precocious little animal he paid a dollar to each time. Thirteen proved to be his unlucky number."

"And thus began your wayward life?"

"And thus it did. I ran away before the law could hang me."

"I knew the first minute I laid an eye upon you that you were the devil's own child."

"Know this, lover, the first time you take a life is the hardest. It gets easier after that."

"You're preaching to the choir. Is that a threat?"

"Take it however you wish . . . but if you cheat on me, well, just say a sharp knife goes in easy."

"I'll keep it in mind."

"Yes, do. How much longer do you think we can live in tall cotton?"

"The rate we're burning through it . . . you and those trunks of fancy clothes . . . another week, maybe two or three before we got to go back to work."

"Hell, that seems a bit drawn out to me. I miss the action of banditry."

"Truth be told, so do I."

"Then let's spend it all and do it quick and get back to the business we both love so well."

"Here, have another glass of champagne."

"Don't mind if I do."

And so they toasted one the other, for life without action soon becomes dull, no matter the quality, no matter how much of breathing the rarefied air of swells one can breathe, or the salt air of the sea, or watching big bears through field glasses that could eat a man in a single sitting, or seeing mountains so lustrous they did not seem real, nor eating oysters on the half shell dipped in garlic butter, nor endless fornication and rivers of expensive booze. None of it compared to thrill of banditry for them.

There was nothing quite like shedding the blood of other men that gave Gypsy Davy and his concubine, Belle Moon, that certain tingle of exotic loftiness and made them feel like little gods.

"You know the meanest trick I think we pulled," said Davy, closing his eyes there on the large bed.

"Hmmm?"

"Wiring that Pinkerton to the fence post and leaving him there for the creatures to get at."

"It was pretty mean, wasn't it? How you reckon he died . . . starvation, thirst, eaten up by insects, wolves, or maybe even struck by lightning?"

Davy shook his head.

"Whatever it was killed him, it was not a slow or easy death, eh? Did you like it, having him chase you through the bush, brazen and naked, knowing he must have thought he was about to catch the brass ring?"

"Oh, dear, yes. It was a clever idea, I must admit. Naughty, too, but admit it . . . you were just a wee bit jealous knowing another man's eyes were seeing me thus." She lifted above him like a she-cat, naked and slim and brown.

"I imagine his bones dangle still and someone will come along and wonder how it was a man came to be wired to a fence post in the middle of nowhere."

"Someone will tell the story and it will grow and grow. They will read the note pinned to his shirt signed with your name and it will become legend."

"Thinking it was me . . . Gypsy Davy . . . who'd been wired to that post."

"The law will have stopped looking for you," Belle said.

"And we'll walk into that bank and out again with bags of money and some might even recognize ol' Davy and say . . . 'He's risen like Jesus, from the dead' . . . and be in awe and wonder."

And the rain fell outside their window, but there wasn't any gloom in their hearts, thinking about robbing that big stone bank with all the windows.

Chapter Nineteen

One came by train, the other by stage.

It was hard to miss a black man nearly seven feet tall wearing leather britches with Liberty dimes sewn down the sides of the legs. He stepped off the chuffing train and through the cloud of steam and stood there like a dark giant looking about. His mood was not fearsome, but his countenance was. Others de-boarding and boarding the train gave him considerable berth. Men averted their eyes when his fell upon them and women nearly fainted from the sight of him.

He carried a brass-fitted Henry rifle he kept well oiled inside a fringed and beaded scabbard and wore a brace of pistols crossed around his waist, butts forward. In his pocket was a telegram from Gypsy Davy of which the big man known back in the pistol barrel of Oklahoma Territory as Blackbird had memorized the few words:

Need a man for a job. Big pay. Come quick if interested. R.S.V.P.

G. Davy, Cheyenne, WT

Already he missed his Osage wife, Jane Two Ponies, but not so much the brood of kids that clamored like the wild little things they were. It was good for a man to get away from all that domestic uproar—especially one who was of a solitary mind and liked his liquor neat and his women silent.

He'd let his hair grow so long he'd had Jane Two Ponies weave it into a rope that fell from under his sweat-stained hat and down the length of his wide back. He made sure he'd not lose the hat by securing it with a stampede string. If you ever lost a hat to the Oklahoma wind, he told Jane, you'll know why I wear this string.

He had not seen Davy in years and the telegram came as a surprise. Now and then he'd read about Davy's exploits in the *Police Gazette* or *Harper's Weekly*. Blackbird prided himself in his ability to read and kept newsprint pasted up everywhere including the two-hole outhouse that had a half moon cut in the door to allow reading light to fall in.

The other striking thing about Blackbird was his eyes: they were a soft gray that looked like gleaming marbles. He figured he got those eyes from somewhere away back when white blood mixed with an ancestor. He did not care much for white men in general, but preferred his own kind or Indians.

The stationmaster said to the porter: "That fellow was to fall into a river with all that hardware he'd drown straight off."

"Looks to me like he'd kill the water fust," the porter replied, privately wishing he was as big and bold as the giant black fellow who stood like a freeborn man upon the station's platform.

When the telegram had arrived, Blackbird was hoeing weeds and sweat dripped into his eyes and he was miserable. The telegram had been a god-send of sorts.

"Where you off to this time?" Jane Two Ponies had asked him when she saw the look of hope light up his gray eyes.

"Where I got to be to feed you and these kids," he had told her, quickly gathering the tools of his trade—the rifle and pistols, bullets and gun belts.

She had already lost two husbands to stormy circumstances—one drowned to death by a pair

155

of drunken cowboys and the other in a fire of uncertain origin. Out of them had come the passel of kids who played most days in the dirt yard or swam naked in a cattle pond, and not a one of them was Blackbird's progeny, but it did not cause him to love them any less or feel any less responsible for feeding them than if they had sprung from his own loins.

"I always worry when you go," she'd said that day.

"Hell, you ought not. Even if I wasn't going, I could fall off the porch and break my neck, or some old fool could ride by and shoot me for the sport. Such are the ways of life, my little peach." It was a stark reminder to her of the two husbands she'd already lost.

She and the youngsters reluctantly carried him to the train station in a buckboard.

"If I ain't back by September, go on and find you a new husband, 'cause it means something bad's happened to me. Otherwise, I'll be back sometime before the corn comes ripe. Can't be nothing shy of a bullet goin' to keep me from coming back to you."

"I wait for you," she said.

So now he was in Cheyenne, looking for Gypsy Davy whilst everyone else was looking at him.

"I ain't no damn' freak," he said to station-master and porter. "So stop staring at me."

"Yes, sir," they replied in unison.

"I'm just goin' to settle on this bench and wait for my friend to show up."

"Yes, sir. Sit long as you want," said the porter.

"I will."

Across the way from the stage line office, lined up in a row, cheek to jowl, stood a hotel, a saloon, a blacksmith shop, a hardware store, a gunsmith, a dentist office, a druggist.

I could stand me a glass of hooch.

Then, while he was contemplating a stroll across the way, in rolled the stage. He sat watching people getting out of it from inside and off the top like fleas leaving a scalded dog, and one of those fleas he recognized as Little Dick Longwinter because Little Dick Longwinter was a hard body to miss with that wine-stain that looked like a map of Europe all over the one side of his face. That as well as the fact that he stood just under five feet tall and had a hump on his back that caused him to look something like a baby buffalo in that moth-eaten buffalo coat he wore summer and winter.

Little Dick's true last name was lost to memory, but he called himself Longwinter because, as he was quick to explain to anyone who cared to listen: "I come close to freezing to death twice up in those high mountains in Colorado, trapped by blizzards so's I can't ever get warm again . . . not truly. You ever come near to death from freezing, you'll understand."

157

Blackbird whistled and Little Dick turned to the sound to discover its source. He trudged over, carrying a knapsack and a gun nearly as long as he was tall—a custom-made German model with which he claimed he could hit a target at half a mile.

"Nobody can see that far," Blackbird had said the first time Little Dick had made his claim, "much less hit anything that far. You'd have to be mighty lucky, Little Dick, and you don't look so lucky to me."

But Little Dick had showed him. He had blown up a prairie dog just minding its own business, eating some wildflowers—bluebells, Little Dick had said they were.

"What you doing here?" Little Dick said, approaching Blackbird on a bench by himself in front of the stationmaster's window.

"I'm waiting for Gypsy Davy to show."

Little Dick set down his knapsack but not his rifle. He did not trust anyone.

"Me, too. Got a telegram says he has big work for me." Little Dick pulled the telegram from somewhere within his moth-eaten curly coat and Blackbird pulled his, too.

"I guess Gypsy must have something big up his sleeve for him to summon us both," Little Dick said.

"Can't be nothing too small," Blackbird said.

"Man sure as hell needs work when he can get it."

"This man sure does."

"Got expenses."

"Got all them kids to feed."

"Whores, here," Little Dick said proudly. "Don't want no wife nor kids, whores do me just fine."

"What's wrong with you? You got the shakes all over."

"It's my blood craving the dope," Little Dick said. "I got in the habit. I got to find me a dope den or I'll shake apart."

"I've heard of dope fiends," Blackbird said. "Knew one or two down in New Orleans. Musicians mostly. Said the dope made 'em play better."

"The dope makes everything better, but it's a bad habit to take up. Won't let you go. Got to keep feeding it or else it will shake you to pieces. I run out of cocaine pills halfway here. You try and find cocaine pills in this wilderness. *Ha!* Good luck with that. But this looks like a town might have a dope den or two. Usually in the China section of town is where I find the best ones. You know where the China section is?"

Blackbird shook his head.

"Just got here myself. Don't know where nothing is except what's across the street."

Little Dick turned and looked.

"Got to be a dope den somewheres. You mind watching my knapsack till I get back?"

"What if Gypsy Davy comes and you ain't here?"

"Tell him to wait."

"He might not."

"Hell with him then. Let him do his own shooting."

"Go on then."

Little Dick was already headed across the street.

Another hour passed and Blackbird kept thinking on that glass of hooch. He favored Kentucky bourbon best. His people were originally from Kentucky. Slaves till the war happened and Lincoln said they could all leave and most of them did—some going to Chicago and others to New York. But what his daddy did was join the Union Army to go fight Indians on the plains as a Buffalo Soldier and got himself shot several times and carried to his eventual grave a stone arrowhead in his leg bone that caused him to limp and moan when the weather turned one way or the other.

Blackbird rose to his feet and stood, tall and straight as a chinaberry tree. Then, remembering, he picked up Little Dick's knapsack and his own Henry rifle and crossed the street and entered the first saloon—The Lazy Sue—and ordered himself a glass of hooch. He sipped it slowly while those around him stared at the sheer size of the man, and stared, too, at those coin-fringed leather britches nobody had ever seen the likes of. And when he finished the first whiskey, he ordered another, figuring if the first one was good, the second should be better, and, by God, it surely was. The liquor settled into his blood like little hot coals.

"You want a black whore?" the barkeep asked. "I know where you can get one."

"I'm a married fool with ten kids," Blackbird said.

"Well, lots of men who visit whores are married," the barkeep said.

"No, suh. I'm loyal to my Jane. I come home with another woman's scent on me, she'd take a hoe to me and feed my parts to the hogs."

"I never served liquor to a man tall as you."

"Lots of men can say that."

It is a conversation that wasn't ever meant to go anywhere so Blackbird let it die then and there, finished his drink, and walked back across the street again.

Little Dick Longwinter sat on the bench, his head lolled down.

"You find you a dope den?" Blackbird said.

Little Dick raised his head, his eyes were dreamy.

"Yes, I did, thank you very much."

"Your eyes is as red as garnets."

Little Dick pointed a lazy finger.

161

"Chinatown is right up that way."

"You still think you can hit something half a mile off?"

A sloppy grin besmirched Little Dick's face, parting his reddish whiskers as if a knife had laid open a place where his mouth could fit in.

"I shoot better when I'm doped up."

Blackbird doubted very seriously whether a man juiced up could even hit himself in the foot with a hammer that way. But he hadn't come all that long way to argue the shooting skills of Little Dick Longwinter, doped or otherwise.

They heard a voice beside them and it was Gypsy Davy, having sneaked up on them like a shadow. The man came and went like a ghost. Always had, always would.

"Welcome, boys, to the neighborhood."

Chapter Twenty

"This here looks like the Queen of Sheba's place," Little Dick Longwinter said when he entered the hotel suite with its Brussels carpets and French furnishings, the ceiling to floor wine-colored drapes, and the carved sideboard with lead-cut crystal decanters of amber liquors.

"It's just a taste of what you all can have, too," Gypsy Davy said, removing his hat and gloves.

Blackbird had to duck his head to enter the

room and again to avoid banging it into the chandelier hanging from the ceiling.

"Them diamonds?" he said questioningly, for he had only once before been in a room with a crystal chandelier—a Texas whorehouse when he was a drover in his long ago youth. The madam had said they were diamonds and being youthful and drunk he believed her.

"Them's crystals," Gypsy said. "All the way from Germany or some such. You boys have a seat. What can I get you to warsh down the dust?"

Little Dick said he'd have a whiskey and Blackbird said: "I always admired champagne."

"Then that's what it shall be," Davy said, and began to pour a round of drinks from a sidebar. Then Belle entered from the adjoining boudoir dressed in a red as blood silk wrap and looking lovely as a princess, and the boys slung off their hats and stood at her entrance like two fine gentlemen. She smiled so brightly the world didn't need a sun.

"Boys, this is Belle . . . my traveling companion and back-up gun. Belle, these are the boys I told you about . . . the tall one is Blackbird and the other is Little Dick. Our new gang."

"I guess I could have figured out which of you was which," Belle said.

Little Dick shuffled his feet, feeling uncomfortable in the presence of so fine a woman because he was not used to any kind of woman

163

who was not by current profession a sporting gal. He felt overly warm inside his heavy coat but he couldn't say if it was the heat of day or the heat of a suddenly arisen passion.

She looked him over carefully and he felt all flushed because of the stain on his face, thinking she was probably put off looking at a man who had been marred at birth and had a hump and stood so short. But she smiled graciously and extended her hand and he wasn't sure if he should shake it or kiss the knuckles, so he did both.

"Why, ain't you quite the gent," she said in a haughty sort of teasing way, and he blushed all the more so that the good side of his face nearly matched its crimson twin.

Then she offered her small delicate white hand to Blackbird and his large hand engulfed hers. She was inwardly mightily impressed at his overall size and wondered if other parts of him matched the rest.

"Pleased to meet you," he said in a deep baritone voice.

Both men stood until Belle seated herself next to Davy before taking their own seats in two chairs upholstered with white brocade cloth and small carved arms trimmed in gold leaf.

"I got me a plan," Gypsy said. "And I need two Turks such as you to help me pull it off."

"Go on with it," Blackbird said. "I din't come all

this way to steal pennies from a dead man's eyes."

Gypsy leaned forward, his long hair hanging loosely around his shoulders like a woman's, his eyes all sparkles. Little Dick thought Davy as handsome as any actor—like that John Wilkes Booth fellow who shot old Abe Lincoln.

"There is a big ol' stone bank in this town and I aim to hit it," Davy continued. "I figure there's at least twenty or thirty thousand dollars sitting in it waiting to be stolen and I aim to steal it. Could even be more . . . can't say for certain since I never robbed no banks before."

"I thought your specialty was as a stage and train robber," Little Dick interjected.

Blackbird remained quiet as a sphinx. He had learned it paid to listen when white men talked of evil things. He hadn't come all this way to offer opinions. Let that be for other men. What he did best, he reckoned, didn't have to do with talk but with action. He caught Belle stealing glances at him as Gypsy and Little Dick conferred on matters at hand.

I could get into trouble easily enough with that one, he thought, *and it won't be from lack of wanting to go the straight and narrow.* But the thought of his wrathful Indian wife, Jane, sent a slight chill through his blood. He believed an Indian woman would cut your throat and let you bleed out while she eats her supper if you give her reason to do it.

"I used to rob stages and trains," Gypsy replied to Little Dick's question. "But I have come to conclude that the real money is in banks and banks don't have nothing pulling them down a highway like a stage or train does. It is always risky robbing a moving thing, and always uncertain as to what the payload might be. I once robbed a stage that didn't have nothing on it but crates of house cats a fellow was taking to sell the whores."

"House cats!" Little Dick said incredulously.

Davy nodded and leaned forward farther still, like a leashed dog straining to get at a meat bone.

"But now a bank is a most certain thing. You boys ever hear of a bank that didn't have no money in it?"

Little Dick shook his head.

"No, sir, I never did. What would be the point?"

"Exactly."

Blackbird continued to sit and say nothing at all, giving away nothing of what was inside his head or otherwise. Belle continued stealing glances. He'd never seen a woman with violet eyes before, white woman or any other kind. Not only would Jane slit his throat, if she knew what he was thinking at present, but Gypsy Davy would shoot him through the eyeballs just for looking at Belle. He had heard stories of Davy's wild rages. A rumor had even been afloat that claimed that Gypsy had killed some of his own gang members.

"Well, I get your point," Little Dick said. "But robbing a bank can prove a tricky endeavor. I mean the whole dang' town will get after you for stealing a bank's money. Look what they did to Jesse and Frank and the Youngers up there in Northfield. Shot 'em to ribbons."

"Bigger the risk, bigger the gain," Gypsy said with a devilish grin. "Ain't that so, Belle?"

She nodded her pretty head, but was more enamored with the prospects of bedding a man the size of Blackbird than of robbing a bank. The tallest man she ever bedded was Ben Poker who was a full head shorter than Blackbird, at least, and that was with his boots on. Ben was a sapling next to the oak, Blackbird. She was feeling a mighty need to climb that tree and swing from it.

"I got it all planned down to the minute," Gypsy continued. "You and me and Blackbird and Belle here makes for a force to be reckoned with. We'll come in armed and dangerous and nobody will stand against us."

Little Dick was still a bit uncertain and spoke his mind.

"I never been in no gang with a woman in it."

"Oh, Belle can shoot the eyes out of a piss ant. She is deadly and her aim is true and she does not quail in the face of danger."

"I do believe I read them same words in a dime novel," Little Dick said. "Spoken from the mouth of Lil' Bess, Queen of the Plains. A DeWitt's."

"Well, if so, then it was stole from me," Gypsy said.

"I could use another shot of this high-price whiskey."

"Help yourself."

Little Dick helped himself, then rejoined the group.

"You boys want to throw in with me and Belle?" Davy asked.

"What's our end of it?" Little Dick said.

Gypsy looked at Blackbird, but Blackbird remained quiet, just minding his own business, listening, taking it all in.

"Give you boys twenty percent each of the haul. A fine sum for less than twenty minutes of work."

"I'd like it better was I to hear fifty percent come out of your yap," Little Dick said, the whiskey making him bolder.

"You'll be waiting a long time to hear that amount come out of my yap or any place else," Davy said. "What say you, Blackbird?"

Blackbird turned his eyes on Davy, but he was still thinking about the trouble he knew he had already let himself in for by what he was thinking about Belle. He knew what it said in the Bible about the mind being willing but the flesh being weak. His flesh was feeling mighty weak.

"Fifty percent sounds good to me, too," he said in response.

"No damn' way. Twenty percent is high as I go. I can always buy other boys with guns."

"But boys ain't men, are they, Blackbird?" Little Dick said. "Not like us 'uns."

"You get what you pay for," Blackbird said.

Gypsy looked consternated. He had not figured on trouble from these two.

"Twenty percent of something is better than fifty percent of nothing. It sounds fair to me for the labor required. I got all the details worked out. All you have to do is walk in and hold your *pistolas* on them clerks and have 'em fill the sacks and ride away."

"Still," said Little Dick, "there is every chance somebody will take it in their heads not to let us get away so easily and will aim to shoot us dead as garbage rats."

"Well, yes, that is part of why I'm offering you boys the twenty percent. You might have to shoot back at them if they try. After all, if it were a waltz, I'd invite women."

"Women!" said Little Dick with a snort.

"Take it or leave it," Gypsy said with finality.

"I'll take it," Blackbird said, for his mind was on more than just stealing bank money, and he could not stand sitting any longer and having Belle look at him slyly like she was. And if he was going to hell, by God, he'd just as soon do it sooner rather than later.

Little Dick conceded as soon as Blackbird did.

"When do we do it?" Little Dick said.

"Tomorrow," Gypsy said. "Bright and early. We'll be the first customers."

"Where we staying tonight?" Blackbird asked.

"Got you boys a room at the end of the hall."

"One room or two?"

"One room."

"I want my own room . . . nothing against you, Little Dick, but I'm a private soul and don't bunk with no mens," Blackbird said.

"OK," Gypsy agreed. "I'll walk down to the lobby and rent another room."

Blackbird threw Belle one more glance and she threw him one back. He felt like he'd swallowed a hot rock that now burned in his gut.

That night she knocked on his door, just like he figured she would, and he rose up eagerly off the bed, the silvery moonlight like a ghost in the room, and answered the door, letting her slip inside.

"He finds you here there'll be some killing going on," he said, but she'd already shucked out of her wrapper and stood before him fully naked and gleaming like one of the alabaster statues he'd seen that time in Italy when he was with that Wild West Combination of Cody's a year or two back.

"Then let there be blood," she said. "For I have come to tempt the tiger."

"Lord, yes, you have."

They got to it right away and it didn't take long to spend their built-up passion. Their fury was such that they looked like the beast with two backs trying to kill something they couldn't quite see in the moon shadows. There was a rustle and clatter of furniture being pushed all around and bedsprings aching and floorboards creaking. Belle yelped and howled like a she-cat and Blackbird grunted like he was hauling ore out of a mine on his back. They heaved and they thrusted until they were spent as shot birds, then laid there, breathing heavily, hearts pounding like angry fists inside their bosoms.

After several minutes they were able to speak.

"What now?" she said.

"You tell me," Blackbird said.

"What are your plans after robbing the bank tomorrow?"

"Plan is to go to Oklahoma."

"Why would anybody want to go to Oklahoma?"

" 'Cause I got a wife and kids back there."

"Send them some money and go with me to San Francisco."

"San Francisco?"

"I always wanted to catch a boat to China and that's where you catch boats to China . . . in San Francisco."

"China?"

"Think of all that money we'd have, the fun

times. They say China's the cheapest place to live, that you can hire a maid for ten cents a week. Why we'd live like royalty, you and me." She sighed.

"You mean keep all of that money for ourselves . . . none for Davy or Little Dick?"

"Yes, all."

"That would mean I'd have to kill Davy and Little Dick?" Blackbird mused.

"Exactly."

"You got this all worked out your own way, don't you?"

"I've been thinking about it ever since I first laid eyes on you," she said.

"You care to let me in on how exactly we goin' to do this?"

So she whispered it to him after straddling his lengthy frame, looking down through her lank hair.

"Well, if that don't put a knot in the tail of the tiger," he said when she finished telling him the plan.

"It does, don't it."

"I'll have to think on it some."

"Don't think too long on it."

And in a moment she was gone, the room empty again, and the places on his back where her claws had raked over him burned like fire, and the places where she had bit through the skin burned like a fire, and all inside his soul burned like fire.

All that money. San Francisco, he thought. *China!* He could almost hear the kids squalling back in Oklahoma. He could see Jane, mad and waiting, knew that she'd wait just so long, then go find herself another man.

The thing was, he still loved her in spite of all the burdens. Love was not so simple a thing to discern the whys and wherefores. On the one hand it seemed to him that life in the pistol barrel had just been repeating itself every day when he was back there with Jane. Whereas life with Belle would be a grand adventure to say the least.

Lord, a mercy, what I goin' do?

Chapter Twenty-One

Walter Fick arose at his usual hour, did stretches in his union suit, bathed from a metal basin of fresh, cold, hand-pumped water, lathered his cheeks, ran a stropped straight razor over them until they were clean and smooth as ivory and just as pale, then dressed in a fine dark suit of clothes over a boiled shirt and celluloid collar, ate a light breakfast of toast and poached egg, coffee mixed with cream and sugar, and kissed his wife Dora good bye before heading to his bank. He had turned fifty-one years old the previous January and was a survivor of Gettysburg where shot and shell had shattered his left arm but had not taken it off completely. Instead, the arm hung uselessly in its sleeve like the dead weight of a window sash.

Walter had learned to adapt to living life with one good arm. He had had to learn to be grateful that it was not his right arm, the one he was accustomed to using, and thus forced to learn to do everything the opposite. Walter Fick had learned to be grateful for what life had given him instead of what it had taken from him.

His home was a nice fine two-story brick house with lots of oak trim and high windows that let in the Wyoming light, summer and winter. He was most proud of his fine library full of leather-bound books—his passion—and a supportive wife who he could count on for his every daily need. And although she had remained barren, and it was a sorrowful thing for him not to have had a son who he could teach the banking business, he felt fortunate to have been delivered—whether divinely or not—his young assistant, John David Moore, a bespectacled boy who had appeared one day out of virtually nowhere asking for a job—"Doing anything, sir."—and said he had walked all the way from Nebraska looking for work. And then he had confessed that he could become almost anything but a farmer. It was as if God had heard Walter's silent grief of being a man without a son and had sent him John David Moore as a replacement.

Walter Fick was most pleased by the boy's

willingness to learn the business of money from the ground up, thus assuring that what Walter Fick had accumulated over the years would not pass to the grave with him. A fine lad, indeed, was John David Moore.

The young man had become like a son to Walter, often taking his evening meals with Walter and Dora in their fine big house, the three of them like family gathered around the long polished dining room table with its high-backed carved chairs and chinaware.

And when Walter entered the bank via a back door, John David Moore was already wearing his eye shade and poring over papers, toting and summing every jot and tittle, leaning over his desk.

"Good morning, Walter."

"Good morning, John." Their greeting was as warm as between father and son.

And within minutes there arrived Sadie Bird and Enid Pierce, two of the bank's tellers who right away began setting up their bank drawers for that day's business.

Enid was a bachelor, like John David, and held private dreams of someday becoming an artist, perhaps living in Europe, hopefully studying under one of the masters, saving a portion of his pay every month for just such a trip.

And Sadie had been widowed from a fairly young age, and for whatever reason had never married again, but instead lived with her good friend, Sally Merriweather, a schoolteacher. The two of them happy as larks, closer than sisters, and occasionally the source of sordid rumors murmured behind the gloved hands of some of the town's biddies who thought it more than a bit unusual for two women to be so openly affectionate. Once or twice Sadie and Sally had been seen holding hands and a schoolboy claimed to have once observed them kissing.

So there they were, the four of them, souls of industry, perhaps not as happy as they could be, but not unhappy, either, when the doors suddenly opened and in stepped three masked men, one of them tall as a poplar tree and black as a moonless night.

"It will do well for you all to not raise a ruckus and put the money into these sacks," one of the bandits said in a quiet, almost humorous manner. The speaker was standing under a high-crowned sombrero with a big kerchief over his face. The tall black man wore leather britches with coins sewn down the legs—Liberty dimes, Walter was sure. And the third fellow was short with a humped back. The one doing the talking took from inside his coat several burlap sacks that once held onions and still had that onion scent about them. He shoved these through the teller cages, while the short man stood guard by the door, having again pulled the green shades down over the window and returned the sign to *CLOSED*.

The tall Negro aimed his pistols at Walter and John David, and said: "You two rascals so much as cough you'll be eating dirt for dinner."

Walter had been robbed once before and had come out of it quite all right. The villains were tracked down, tried, and sent to prison, and most of the money recovered. So he was not overly worried as to the outcome of the situation and told the others: "Co-operate with these men."

By all accounts, things were moving quite smoothly with the burlap sacks having been stuffed with paper money and silver. But Davy noted the heavy steel door of a large vault that had remained closed.

"Open that safe," Davy ordered.

"It's on a time lock," Walter explained. "It will not open until nine-thirty . . . half an hour from now."

"Time lock? Well, set the time to now and open it."

"I can't."

Davy, not being experienced at bank robbery, had not heard of time locks and safes that would not open until a certain hour. He saw it as a ruse, a way for the tight-fisted banker to keep all the money.

"To hell, you say!" He stuck the barrel of his pistol to Walter's knob of a head, cocking back the hammer as he did so. "Is your brains worth that money?"

"No, sir. But I can't open that safe until nine-thirty."

"Nine-thirty is too damn' long to wait."

"I'm sorry. . . ."

Whether he meant to or not, Davy's finger twitched on the trigger and the pistol shot sounded like the crack of thunder in a summer storm.

The shot knocked Walter off his feet and to the floor where he lay still as stone. The shooting was so unexpected that John and the others jumped nearly a foot. And Sadie dribbled a bit in her bloomers.

"We might just as well kill them all," Little Dick shouted, standing by the doors, "else they'll identify us and we'll be hanged!"

Davy now blamed his gun for the unexpected turn of events. The parts of his gun had become loose over time and use, a condition he was well aware of and had been meaning to have fixed, but hadn't yet, so consumed had he been with Belle Moon and his own lust for her. It was not the killing that irked him so much as the error and the dead man's bloody offal splattered over his handsome face.

He swiped at his eyes with the bandanna, then examined it.

"Oh, hell," he said in disgust, and shot John David through the middle, felling him like a young sapling clipped by a sharply swung axe.

Little Dick stepped forward and shot quiet Enid

Pierce, whose mouth formed an O at the sight of John David lying at his feet, a ribbon of blood from the body grown as fat as a red worm. Enid stumbled halfway across the room, grasped at wood boxes of receipts, pulling them down with him as he crumpled. Pieces of paper fluttered down around him like wounded birds. His last thoughts were of cafés in Paris, France.

The only innocent left standing was Sadie Bird who had never done a wrong thing to anybody. Her handsome young husband, Tom, had fallen into an abandoned mine and broken both legs and by the time he was found it was too late. And so she had grieved as any wife would grieve, and was comforted by her friend Sally, the school-teacher, and their friendship became something deeper than mere friendship in the passage of a single lonely night. And thus Sally had replaced Tom in Sadie's affections.

Now Sadie stared into the muzzles of the strangers' guns, having witnessed the death of all three of her friends and co-workers and could only assume her own time had come. She prayed it was not true, that God would save her, but would He, really, after what had transpired between Sally and her?

"Somebody shoot this one," Gypsy ordered.

But Little Dick shook his head.

"I can't shoot no woman."

"Then you do it," Gypsy said to Blackbird.

"No," Blackbird said. "I ain't never killed no woman before and I ain't about to start this day. You wants her killed, you better get to it."

Everyone by that time was nervous: robbers and the remaining victim. Surely others would soon arrive to come see what all the shooting was about, drawn by the sound of gunfire like cats to the scent of fish.

Gypsy thumbed back the hammer of his iron, aimed it at Sadie, but when he pulled the trigger, the gun misfired. He took it as a sign among signs that it was not meant to be; fate had dealt the hand it had dealt and he'd best play it as it was.

Looking into those faded blue eyes, eyes like those of his own ma, the only part of her that he remembered, he lowered his piece.

"Let's go!" he yelped, and all three turned and slipped out the door and onto their mounts being held by Belle Moon who did not require explanation about what had taken place inside the bank. Belle figured the boys had killed everyone at Davy's request, because that was how Davy played things: no witnesses.

"It sounded like a war in there," she said as they kicked their mounts into a run. "Couldn't you have raised *more* of a ruckus!" The sarcasm was not lost on Davy.

Townsfolk had already started to approach the brick bank cautiously. Some were also armed, but uncertain and cautious.

"We best skedaddle before these sodbusters wipe us all out like they did the Youngers!" Little Dick yelped.

"We best," Blackbird said.

They spurred their mounts like there was candy waiting for them at the finish line of a race.

Off they raced to the north where Davy had previously arranged to lay low overnight at an old reprobate's shack, where, if not discovered, they would ride off again at first light. Only as before, Davy had conceived an alternative plan that he had not revealed to the boys, and this time not even to Belle. A plan that would leave Little Dick and Blackbird floating on the river Styx, dead as doorknobs.

He'd have the old fool and his loutish sons kill Little Dick and Blackbird in their sleep. He and the crazed old man had already agreed on a price along with a night's billet. A bullet to the brain ought to do it nicely enough, Davy had told the old bastard.

Then he and Belle would go wherever there was a riverboat heading north or south and ride it to the river's mouth or headwaters and depart for parts unknown.

He had always delighted himself with what he considered ingenious plans.

But unknown to Davy, Belle had plans of her own that involved only her and Blackbird—at least for the present—until she grew weary of him as she knew that she would over time. Men were just creatures that soon lost their attraction, and like money or hats or shoes there was always a need to replace them with regularity. She'd like to go to China first, and then travel to England to see Queen Victoria—at least a glimpse—and other forays such as visiting the pyramids. She had become absolutely weary of the West and its characters, such as Gypsy Davy. She already had assured herself that even Blackbird would wear thin in a month or two of steady congress with him. Beyond the fact that he was large and strange—new territory for her—she sensed him to be dull-witted and much like a homing pigeon with a homing pigeon's instinct for returning to the familiar.

Hadn't he already spoken of his wife and children? It was a dead giveaway that he had little or no imagination. Well, let him return once she had finished having her fling with him. But without a red cent to sustain him. She planned on keeping the whole take. And Little Dick was having his own problems: stomach cramps, something he ate the previous night—perhaps the green chili, two full bowls.

They rode the horses nearly down trying to put distance between themselves and whatever posse might be formed by the good citizens of Cheyenne. Then they turned off the main road and up a back trail to the shack the reprobate and his dull-witted sons inhabited like a brood of opossums.

Gypsy had it all planned.

Belle was thinking: *You'll make a pretty little corpse.*

Little Dick was trying not to crap in his pants.

And Blackbird couldn't be certain of anything.

Chapter Twenty-Two

Jack Corn had a brood of ill-tempered boys who he sent forth on regular forays to rob and steal whatever they could: chickens, hogs, lumber, crops, and anything that wasn't nailed down and some things that were. There were five in all: Alonzo, Tobe, Hector, Warren, and Brazil, the one they called Peckerwood.

They were clearly cut from the old man's cloth—all with long noses and close-set eyes and ears like jug handles. They spent their free time cursing and fighting one another like tomcats. They were poor and mostly went about barefooted and raggedly clothed. And when they weren't stealing or fighting amongst themselves, they would sit in the shade of a tree or corncrib and drool over renderings of females in the Sears, Roebuck catalogue. They would fumble with their privates, then sleep like lazy raccoons.

Jack Corn would haul them to Cheyenne every

three months or so and pay a crib girl with broken front teeth $5 for a turn with himself and all his boys. Jack Corn made sure he got first turn with her, then passed her to his brood, the eldest first right down to the youngest, Brazil.

In spite of his imperfections as a human, Jack Corn kept a pocket Bible from which he read almost any time he wasn't fornicating, dealing in stolen goods, or kicking his offspring into action. The stealing he sent his boys to do was, as he saw it, simply a way to teach them to subsist on their own once he had passed to the great beyond. In other words, Jack saw himself as a mostly good Christian with a few flaws but doing the best he could, given the circumstances.

"I will be with Jesus, one day soon enough," he was fond of telling his brood. "And you boys will need to be prepared to forage on your own oncet I'm passed over. You got no education, and, even if you did, where would you put it to use on this rough frontier?"

The late Mrs. Corn had been a woman given to unexplained bouts of the vapors and would stay for days inside a locked room reading poetry to herself. She came to believe that she was the Empress Cleopatra and grew increasingly insane over the years.

Jack Corn grew so afraid of her that he slept with a loaded six-gun under his pillow because he could hear her roaming through the house in the night, rattling pots and pans and talking to herself—spouting that poetry she was so fond of reading, and calling out the name of Marc Antony. She got so bad Jack Corn swore her eyes glowed red in the dark.

He aimed to have her committed to an insane asylum he'd heard about in Lincoln, Nebraska, but somehow she intuited he was about to do something with her and wandered away from the house to a rock outcropping, found a big red rattler, and carried it back to the house where Jack and her sons, around a table, were eating a supper of stew made from the butchered meat of a stolen goat.

She burst into the room and stood there, babbling, holding the snake, and all of those who were eating dived under the table, Jack Corn disconcerted that he had forgotten the six-shooter he kept under his pillow. He'd have shot the snake or her or both.

The snake had become highly agitated and struck her twice, once on the cheek and once on the neck, but still she held it, her eyes ablaze for a moment longer before tossing it aside where Alonzo beat it to death with his chair, busting the chair apart in doing it.

"Mama, are you crazy!" shouted the youngest boy, Brazil. He alone among the others favored her the most with his fair and freckled skin and bluebird eyes. He also had her sensitivities and his siblings had nicknamed him Peckerwood because he was not as rough and tumble or as coarse as the rest.

The woman, twice bitten, stood tottering, looking at Jack so longingly and lovingly it scared him. Droplets of blood the size and color of rubies slid down her cheek and neck. Then she collapsed and suffered greatly for seven hours more before she gasped and died. Jack Corn had his boys dig her a grave out back of the house, down the slope, away from the source of well water, while he sat solemnly looking on and sipping from a jug of potato whiskey. Some parts of him were sorry to see her go. She was always willing to give her body to him when he came to her in the night up until she started to go crazy. She was also a fair cook and could sew, milk a cow, when they had a cow to milk, and churn butter. She kept their clothes washed and the house swept out and bathed herself every Sunday so that she smelled fresh as mown grass. Jack knew he would also miss her fine singing voice and the way she could play the piano with both hands and not just one. The boys had come home with an old upright roped in the back of their wagon one day. She was so glad to see it she never questioned its source, although it looked similar to the one a neighbor had in her parlor.

But then, there were other parts of Jack Corn that were glad his wife had passed over. It would mean saving him a long and arduous trip hauling her all the way to Lincoln, Nebraska to have her committed. For many times he had thought to himself: *What do you do with a crazy woman? They ain't like a dog you can run off or just shoot.*

It had been pure coincidence that the last time he'd taken his brood of boys into Cheyenne to visit the crib gal that he'd run into an old *compadre*—Gypsy Davy—a boy who'd been a member of Chug Matthew's band of border men along with Jack Corn back in the old days. Gypsy was so young in those days he couldn't even grow hair on his face. But the boy had showed plenty of promise as a bandit. He had the coldness of winter rain in his blood.

Jack had just finished with the crib gal and left his boys with her whilst he sauntered over to the Inter-Ocean Hotel and bought himself a bottle and was standing there, minding his own business, having at the free luncheon, when Gypsy came in with a beautiful woman. Gypsy strutted as if in rarefied air and wore two guns and a big sombrero.

They'd greeted each other with a bit of trepidation, but then warmed to each other after a few drinks had been shoved back and forth between them. Jack Corn could hardly take his eyes off that milk white cleft that was between Belle's ample bosoms. If she'd been a slab of bacon and he a hound, he'd have scarfed her down right then and there.

The two desperados caught up each other on their own private histories with Davy ending by saying: "You say you have a place a few miles from here back off the beaten track?"

"Yes, yes. Me and them boys of mine. Why you ask?"

"I've got something I'm working on," Davy said. "Might need a place to stay overnight, me and some of my pals, if you get my meaning."

"I don't care to know your meaning," Jack Corn said. "How much you offering to pay for a night's stay . . . with the assurance you'll have full protection from me and my boys should trouble come?"

"I'd pay a handsome price for that sort of assurance."

They agreed on $100.

"Done," said Jack Corn, spitting in his hand before he offered it to Davy to shake.

Davy and Jack shook on it, and Jack drew him a map on how to get there.

"Maybe in a week or so, look for us," Davy said.

"I'll keep both eyes and a peck of potatoes peeled," Jack said, seeing everything in life to a degree in terms of either humorous or tragic consequences.

Then Jack started to go, but Davy stopped him by tugging on his sleeve.

"What?" Jack said. "Don't tell me you changed your mind already."

"No. But I was thinking, I might want more than a place to stay overnight. How do you and those boys of yours feel about making some extra money beyond just a night's rent?"

Jack said: "I'm all ears."

And Gypsy hinted the extra money might have something to do with a little killing and Jack didn't so much as flinch as he said: "Anything is possible if the price is right."

"I'll let you know," Gypsy said.

And so on a buzzing warm early afternoon Jack Corn saw the rise of dust a mile or so from the house and figured it was Davy having come at last with his little band of cut-throats and thieves, whoever they might be, and it was OK with him. But mostly he was hoping that the woman named Belle Moon would be among his overnight guests. She made the broken-tooth crib gal look like a sack of cobs.

And $100—just for letting them stay the night —and, Gypsy had even hinted there could be more, the price of murder being what it was. $100 sure could buy some good liquor and a better class of whore next time he took his progeny into town to have the edge rubbed off them.

He stood and stretched, and Tobe, the middle boy, who had been resting there in the shade of the overhang, sat up and said: "Somethin's coming."

Jack Corn ordered Tobe to go kill and dress two yard chickens and peel some potatoes and get a pot of victuals going.

"Why me, why not Alonzo or Hector or one of them?"

" 'Cause I told *you* to do it!" Jack Corn kicked him in the rump out from under the shade. And Tobe rubbed his rump while going off in search of two yard chickens to kill for supper.

Gypsy and the others rode up and halted their lathered mounts there at the altar of Jack Corn's abode, such as it was. Jack looked over the two men with Davy closely, then said to Davy: "We need to talk about something in private." Belle was dressed in men's clothes this time and a disappointment for Jack to have to gaze at her dressed that way.

Davy dismounted and followed Jack inside the low-ceilinged *ranchero*. The interior was as cool and dim as a cave and sour with the scent of men living alone for a long time without the cleaning hand of a woman.

"What is it?" Davy said.

"You din't say nothing about no nigger."

"Nigger?"

"What else would you call that big galoot with the leather britches sitting out there on thet horse?"

"That's Blackbird," Gypsy said. "I thought you knew Blackbird from back in the old days, or at least had heard of him?"

"I don't know nothing about what you're talking about. But there ain't no nigger sleeping in my house and eating at my table."

"When'd you get so high and mighty?"

"I'll run him off myself personal," Jack Corn threatened.

"You ain't heard all of the plan yet," Davy said.

"You best get to telling it to me then afore I go and shoot that black son-of-a-bitch."

Gypsy grinned.

"How'd you like to do it and get paid to do it?"

"Now you're talking my lingo."

"And the other one, too, Little Dick?"

"Bingo! Put the money in my hand right now."

Davy counted $200 extra from what he took out of his pockets. Jack counted it out.

"A hundred apiece," said Davy in a low voice. "But I figure once they are asleep. It will be easy."

"Tell that big black son-of-a-bitch he can come in."

"I reckon," Davy said.

The whole time they sat around the table eating, all Jack Corn could do was think about what Belle would look like without those men's clothes.

Belle did her best to ignore the hungry stares of the Corn clan. It was the first time in her life she'd felt nervous around men.

Later she said to Davy as they walked out to the privy together: "Those boys look like they'd like to cut me up into pieces and chew all the meat off my bones."

"We'll be gone first light," he assured.

"I'm not sleeping in there with them all around."

"Where will you sleep then?"

"Out here somewhere."

"Don't be foolish. Let them half-wits sleep on the ground and you and me in a nice bed."

"What if they try something?"

"I'll put a bullet in them."

Blackbird and Little Dick Longwinter sat outside, smoking in the shadows of the night.

"You see the way that son-of-a-bitch was looking at me," Blackbird said.

"How was he looking at you?"

"Like he hated Africans."

"You ain't no African. You're from Oklahoma, I thought you said."

"All black men are descended from Africa."

"Then where are all white men descended from?"

"Europe, I reckon."

"Hell, maybe I'm Italian or French."

"Maybe you are . . . somewhere back in your blood."

"Wonder upon wonders. Here all this time I thought I was just nobody at all . . . just a man who went around doing what I needed to do. Now I find out I could be Italian or French. Hell, who's to say I ain't descended from some king or something?"

"I don't trust those white suckers inside," Blackbird said.

"That one they call Peckerwood is sure enough a queer-acting duck," Little Dick replied.

"Sissy little bastard."

"Never seen none no sissier."

"I got a feeling about all them Corns."

"What kind of feeling?"

"A bad one."

"I wished you hadn't told me that."

"Why not?"

"Now I got a bad feeling about them, too."

"Best keep one eye open when you sleep tonight."

"They might be thinking the same with us."

"I hope they are."

Night descended, and, even as Gypsy was working over Belle, she trying to be quiet and not moan for fear she'd stir up a hornet's nest of lust among the Corns, Gypsy was planning murder in his heart.

And not just the murder of Blackbird and Little Dick, either.

Chapter Twenty-Three

We did our best to rest all night on the hardwood bench but there wasn't any comfort to it. Somewhere in the dark, pistol shots awakened me from a light drowse and I sat up, and so did Dew Hardy.

"What you think that was all about?" he said.

"I don't know, but I sure wish I had a match so I could roll a shuck and smoke it." Inwardly the craving for whiskey had returned, too, but I fought it hard.

"What you thinking about?" I said, seeing Dew Hardy's grim face in the moonlight.

"I was thinking of a house looking over the ocean," he said.

"Which one, the Atlantic or Pacific?" I said.

"Pacific."

"I never seen the ocean myself," I confessed.

"I seen the one but not the other. They say you can see whales in the Pacific certain times of the year. You ever see a whale?"

"I heard they were big."

"I heard if you was to stand one on its tail, their head would reach the roof of a three-story building. I'd like to see a fish that big."

"Sounds like maybe you ought to have become a sailor instead of a detective," I said.

"It sure would have been a lot more romantic of a life. Probably safer, too, as it's proving to be so far. I'd never gotten wired to a fence post and left for dead."

"Well, I don't know. If you're on some ship out in the middle of the ocean and it gets a hole in it . . . that don't sound like a much better deal to me. I'll take my chances here on dry land, thank you very damn' much."

It was like most of our conversations; it wasn't going anywhere important. There's nothing quite so onerous as the drag of a long night waiting for something.

"Have you thought how you want to play it when we catch Davy and Belle?" Dew Hardy said.

"I was thinking just head on . . . do what needs doing," I said.

"And now?"

"I guess some of my hate's let up for what they did."

"Let up?"

It was true. There was something about being in that infirmary and the kindness of strangers that had changed me in no way that I could explain to anyone, most especially a fellow like Dew Hardy.

"Hate and anger are hard for me to hold onto any more . . . not like when I was a younger man," I said by way of trying to explain it. Some of it, too, I suspected had to do with the feeling that since Ophelia and my boy had passed that nothing seemed all that important to me. My temper was like a struck match head that flared, stayed lit for a flash, then burned itself out.

That was how I'd come to feeling about catching Davy and Belle. Catch them, sure, but then take them to the jail and let the law deal with them. *Enough blood's been shed to fill a rain barrel.*

"They probably won't give you no choice in the matter," Dew Hardy said, "knowing them two and how desperate they are."

"If they don't, they don't," I said.

"You think you could do it . . . shoot a woman if you had to?"

I shifted the shotgun from across my legs and let it rest on the bench. I knew what a powerful ally it was, how it could shred flesh and shatter bone.

"I'll do what I have to do, but to tell the truth, my mood ain't for blood if it don't have to be," I said. "I think, given the chance, Gypsy and Belle will see the wisdom of not arguing with one of these." I patted the shotgun's stock.

"You're thinking of taking them in, ain't you? Just arresting them and clapping them in some old jail and letting the law handle it . . . after what they did to you and them others."

"Seems to me you're the one ought to be

thinking about the law, you being a Pinkerton, having sworn to something or other, I'm not sure what, when you took the badge."

Dew Hardy brought the badge from his pocket and held it in the palm of his hand and stared at it, the moonlight dull against the nickel it was stamped from.

"Shit, men have sold their souls for a lot less than what I aim to get off Davy when we catch him."

"Whatever made you think you wanted to become a Pinkerton in the first place?"

"Hell, that's an easy one. It was a job."

We heard a dog bark somewhere off in the dark, the racket of its bark echoing against the wooden buildings.

"You ever heard of Charlie Siringo?" Dew Hardy asked.

"Yeah, I've heard of him."

"Now there's a son-of-a-bitch who takes his detective work to heart." Dew Hardy snorted. "Told me once there wasn't no kind of man he couldn't track. Said he could find an African in a mine shaft."

"You believe he could?"

"I think he could, yes, sir, I do."

Again, our palaver died like an untended campfire. We dozed and awoke and fell asleep again, restless as sore-footed cats.

"What time they say the train gets in?" Dew

Hardy asked as the first gray of a new morning rimmed the horizon.

"That old fellow never said . . . just said it got in early."

"You reckon we got time to walk up the street and get some coffee and eggs and bacon before it pulls in?"

"I reckon," I said. "You reckon you still got enough from the sale of that stolen horse to go us that sort of breakfast?"

"I reckon probably so," Dew Hardy said. "But that horse wasn't so much stolen as it was borrowed, just remember that."

"It ain't up to me to say whether it was stolen or not. I don't know why we're sitting here. I reckon, if that train's like most, it blows its whistle when it comes in."

"I reckon so."

We walked up the street to a café and sat down at a table feeling wrung out, our legs sprawled out from the table and didn't even look at the chalk board but ordered bacon and eggs, flapjacks and coffee and wolfed it down when it was set before us.

"You wouldn't happen to have a kitchen match, would you?" I asked the waiter when he came to take our dishes.

"I might," he said.

"I'd appreciate one to smoke me a shuck."

The waiter went away and returned again with

a match and set it down next to my coffee cup. I rolled myself a thin little shuck that I proceeded to smoke with great pleasure, having waited so long to smoke it.

"I guess I misjudged you," I said to the Pinkerton, exhaling a stream of smoke.

"How's that?"

"I figured you for a no good son-of-a-bitch when you quit on me. But you proved me wrong, hauling my shot-up hide to that infirmary, and for that I thank you."

"Well, I'm half out of my mind some days . . . it's this job, I reckon is what it is. Always on the move, always looking for trouble, always sleeping on the ground and lonesome will do such things to a man's mind. It's easy to lose yourself in this world."

We heard the far cry of the train whistle and Dew Hardy paid the tab and we walked out together down the mostly empty street toward the train station, and stood watching until it appeared as a black dot on the horizon, then larger and larger, chuffing steamy smoke from its stack.

"There she is," Dew Hardy said, and bought two tickets from the stationmaster when he opened his window.

Dew Hardy and I took seats across from each other in the cramped passenger car and waited for the train to depart.

And whilst waiting a soft rain began to fall.

Water drops dribbled down the window glass like tears. And the train shivered beneath our feet like a quivering animal, anxious to go.

"I always liked trains," Dew Hardy said.

"I thought you liked ships?"

"I like them, too. Anything beats riding a horse in my book."

"Nothing beats riding one in mine."

"I read recently that they got some sort of locomotion machine back East."

"A what?"

"A machine you ride in with an engine. Two people can sit in it and go anywhere."

I said: "How's that ever going to work?"

Dew Hardy shook his head.

"I don't know, but you know they already got electric lights in El Paso."

"So I've heard."

"It's progress, I guess."

"Some things I'd just as soon not be around to see."

"You're old-fashioned for a man so young," the Pinkerton said.

"I ain't all that young," I said. "Besides, I've seen about all I care to. I've seen enough, I mean."

"Nine more years it will be a new century, you ever think of that?"

"I try not to think too much about that."

"You like the old ways," he said. "Not me."

I watched the rain.

"Well, by God, I can't wait for the new century to get here," Dew Hardy said.

"Is that because you're aiming to be rich with all that stagecoach gold and live in a house overlooking the ocean?"

"Yes, and I'd like to own one of those locomotion machines."

"If they don't hang you for horse thieving first."

"Like I said, it was a borrowed horse . . . she lent it to me."

"I bet she's not untied herself even yet."

Dew Hardy smiled a devilish smile.

"Maybe not. I tied her up pretty damned good."

The whistle blew sharply and the car shuddered, lunged, shuddered again, and then began moving steadily but slowly at first, not hitting its stride until the town had become lost in the dreary gray of rainfall, time and motion carrying me and Dew Hardy to maybe our final destiny.

Chapter Twenty-Four

The flyer rolled into Cheyenne just after noon and we stepped off through a cloud of steam, glad to stretch our legs. Folks stared at the shotgun I was carrying. It felt like part of my arm by now.

"My, my," Dew Hardy said, looking around. "This place has grown some since I was last here in pursuit of a bunko artist and counterfeiter named Bunny Snow. Caught him taking a bubble bath with a married woman and nobody was more surprised than him."

"Let's go see the local law," I said, and asked a porter if he knew where the local law office was. He pointed a bony finger toward the town proper.

"Right on up the street three blocks and take a left," he said.

And up the street we went like the two lost and horseless men we were, tramping through the already hardening muck from overnight rain but now baking under a blazing sun. We found the lawman's office easy enough.

Out front a dozen men sat horses, armed with rifles, shotguns, pistols, anything that would fire a bullet. It was easy to see that most of them were not hardened manhunters by the way they were dressed: paper collars and straw hats.

A frosty-eyed man stood before them, holding court.

"We need to find those murdering dogs who killed our people and I ain't overly choosy about what we all do to them when we *do* find them. Blood has been spilled this day and I aim we spill more of it, but this time theirs and not our own."

He was a little long in the tooth, with a shock of white hair that fringed from under his abused Stetson, and had the posture of an old fence post. His appearance and basso voice gave the impression of Moses shouting from the mountain-top.

Dew Hardy and I stood on the fringe, listening, then the Pinkerton said: "I know that fellow. His name is Bob Coin and he was once a Texas Ranger, and, when he was with that organization, he had a reputation of being judge and jury."

He seemed to be revered by the crowd of men who sat their horses being hoorayed on by him. He might have seemed old, but I had the impression he was hard as hickory itself and preferred to keep things simple. Why waste time with a judge and jury?

"Sounds like we might have got here too late," Dew Hardy said.

"You think it's Gypsy Davy they're after?"

"Who else but Gypsy Davy would cause a ruckus that would raise a posse this big?"

"Pardon me," I said, working my way past the mounted men and tapping the old marshal on one bony shoulder. "But what's gone on here?"

Those ancient lawman eyes went first to my weapon, and then to me.

"Our bank was robbed this morning and the folks working it were shot like dogs, all but for one woman who, I suppose by dint of some odd compassion, they let live. You boys want to join our posse?"

"We've got no horses," Dew Hardy chimed in.

He looked past me to the Pinkerton with the same steady gaze of suspicion.

"Well, we ain't got no time to wait until you get some," the old man said, then untied his mount from the hitch rail, and threw himself into the saddle, spry as a younger man, and led the bunch off to the north, their rifles and shotgun barrels poking the air like quills.

"Let's find that woman they didn't kill," I said.

After a bit of asking around, we learned of her residence—a small house a block off the main drag with flower boxes and a picket fence.

Once we arrived, I stepped up and knocked on the wood door and was soon greeted by a large busty woman with a bun of iron gray hair and apple cheeks.

"Yes?" she said, looking me up and down with the same suspicion the lawman had.

"Are you the lady from the bank that was robbed this morning?"

She shook her head.

"Not me. Sadie," she said.

"I'd like a word with her," I said.

"She's in quite a state. I'd just as soon she not be disturbed."

"I'm looking for the men who shot up the place," I said. "It won't take but a moment. One question and then we're gone."

She looked at Dew Hardy, then called back in the room.

Another woman appeared. She was petite and skittish with mud brown eyes and quite pretty in spite of her sorrowful countenance. She stood close to the larger woman, almost like a child standing next to her mother.

"Pardon me, ma'am, but I understand you were in the bank that was robbed this morning," I said.

She remained silent. I guess she could still see the dead, the pools of blood, and hear the bang of pistols being fired off. She had that sort of look.

Dew Hardy stepped forward and said: "Was one wearing a big sombrero?"

"Oh, God . . . ," she muttered.

"And had a good-looking woman with him?"

She shrugged.

"I did not see a woman," she said.

"But a big sombrero nonetheless?"

"Yes."

"It's him, like I said," Dew Hardy told me.

"Thank you, ma'am," I said.

We walked back to the town.

"What now?" Dew Hardy said. "Any ideas how we're going to catch up to them horseless?"

"You got any money left?"

"Not enough to buy a pair of nags."

"How much?"

Dew Hardy counted his dough.

"Eighteen dollars and thirty-two cents total."

We stood, studying the streets. They seemed

calm, considering. Still there was commerce, wagons driven by teamsters, horseback riders, cabs. Funny, I thought, but a slaughter can take place and the world hardly pauses to draw a breath. Life goes on without you no matter who you are.

"I could stand a stiff one," Dew Hardy said, pointing across the street to a saloon.

The truth was, I could stand a stiff one, too. The problem was, could I keep it down to just one and not two or three or more?

We stepped in and stood at the bar. The place was quiet. I figured most of those who might have been patrons were in that posse. The barkeep asked what we were having and Dew Hardy said—"Anything but lemonade."—which caused the barkeep to blink. He was missing a thumb on his right hand.

"Make it two whiskies," I said, "and only two."

He poured and set them before us, and Dew Hardy paid.

"You boys going after the bank robbers?" the barkeep asked. "I hear there is a one thousand dollar reward on them. I'd go myself, but Mister Orvis wouldn't like me closing the bar."

He was young and way too eager.

"Best you take Mister Orvis's advice, son," I said.

We tossed back our drinks and I said to the Pinkerton: "Come on."

We walked back outside.

"You come up with a plan yet?" Dew Hardy said.

"I guess we'll have to borrow some horses," I said.

"Borrow some? Who is going to let two yahoos they've never seen before borrow their horses?"

"I guess whoever is busy doing something," I said, looking up the street at a hitch rail with three saddle horses tied up in front of a mercantile.

"You mean steal them?" Dew Hardy said.

"Something you're pretty good at," I said.

"I told you already I didn't steal Miss Winesop's horse. She lent it to me in good faith."

"So you keep saying. Those two on the left seem best. I'll take the dun and you take the sorrel."

"Suppose I prefer the sorrel over the dun?"

Only two fools would argue who was going to steal which horse, I thought.

"Take whichever damned horse you want, but just take one and let's ride."

An hour later we caught up to the posse. It was resting beneath a grove of chinaberry trees where a creek cut through and the switch grass was as tall as a man's knees. Most of them were reclining in the grass and smoking, but the old lawman stood apart from the others, just staring off. They had run their mounts hard and they were all lathered with sweat, their tails swishing flies off their quivering hides.

"I see you boys found you some horses," the old star packer said when we rode up.

"We felt it our duty to help you catch whoever robbed your bank," Dew Hardy said quite innoently.

"Why is that? That you feel it your duty?" The old man had that curious lawman's nature: distrustful of strangers. "You ain't from Cheyenne . . . least I never seen you around these parts. So why pitch in?"

Dew Hardy shrugged, then produced his Pinkerton badge.

"I am a detective and sworn to uphold the law and bring to justice lawbreakers. Besides, the man you're after is the same one we've been after. His handle is Gypsy Davy."

The aged marshal eyed the badge, leaned forward, and spat, striking a grasshopper eating the blade of grass it clung to. The spit knocked it off.

"Well, ain't that something," the old man said. "I reckon I'm supposed to be impressed. But what I want to know is, who are them others with him?"

"One's a woman," Dew Hardy said. "Belle Moon. You ever heard of them?"

The old man nodded his head.

"Yes, I've heard of Davy, but not Belle Moon."

"Well then you know what sort of fellow you're after," Dew Hardy said.

By now the others had pricked up their ears and were curious.

"I don't have to know the names to know how bloody they are," the lawman said. "They shot in cold blood three of our finest citizens. You know them is some hard customers who would do a thing like that . . . murder unarmed men. Sadie said they wanted what was in the vault but that the vault would not open and so they shot everyone to rags except her." He shook his head and spat again. "Why is it they let her live? Hell if I know. I guess I'll ask 'em just before I kick the horses out from under them with a rope around their necks."

I found all the conversation a waste of time.

"While you all are taking your leisure, they're putting daylight between you," I said.

The lawman tossed me a hard look.

"Don't try and tell me my business, son. I've been doing this a long time."

"Maybe we'll just ride on ahead," I said.

"You do whatever you like."

"I'm told there is a reward for them," Dew Hardy said.

"Why, yes," the lawman said, patting the butt of his pistol. "This here."

We rode away.

"I don't think that bunch, except for that

lawman, could catch a cold," I said to the Pinkerton. "And even if they did catch them, I don't believe any of them would stand up to a gunfight except for him."

We kept a steady pace so as not to ruin our mounts but pushed them as hard as we dared.

"These are some good horses," Dew Hardy said.

"For stolen stock they ain't too bad."

"What do you think that hard ol' hickory would do to us if he knew we stole these horses?"

"Same thing he'd do to Davy and them," I said.

"I reckon."

"Keep a sharp eye in case they turn off the road."

"I'm all about tracking a man," Dew Hardy said.

"You can prove it to me."

"I will."

"Talk is cheap."

He looked at me.

"Ain't it, though."

In spite of everything, I sort of took to the son-of-a-bitch.

Chapter Twenty-Five

"Hell," Dew Hardy said just as the evening sky became streaked with something akin to the color of watered blood. We heard quail cooing off in the sage. "Following these *hombres* is about the easiest thing I ever did. Four fast horses on this road tearing up clots. Look yonder how them tracks meander off down that trace yonder."

I turned off where he pointed and he came up alongside me.

"We could ride ourselves right into an ambush," he said.

"I reckon that's the chance we'll have to take."

"What if they stand and fight?"

"Then I guess somebody is going to get killed."

"I like that idea, but only if it ain't me that's the one who gets killed."

We followed the trace down over rough low hills, the evening air closing around us.

"We could get lost in the coming dark," Dew Hardy said.

"These horses will see well enough."

"You've a mighty big trust in horses."

"More so than in most men I've known."

An hour more and we saw lights on in a house that sat low in a narrow valley surrounded by the dark shapes of trees.

"You reckon . . . ?" Dew Hardy said in a low voice.

"It would seem about right, wouldn't it?"

We pulled up, dismounted.

"We'll leave the mounts here," I said. "There's bound to be other horses down there and I don't want them talking back and forth to each other."

We tied the reins to a low branch of a tree.

"What if they run off?"

"Easy come, easy go," I said.

We eased our way toward the cabin, our boots crunching on the caliche. The darkness had now surrounded us, but a moon had lifted into the night sky and cast down a ghostly light over everything.

When we reached the lip of an overhang, we could see better the squares of yellow light falling through the windows of the cabin. There were some shapes of men standing outside, smoking, the glow of their cigarettes like fireflies. We were close enough to hear their muted voices. Then we saw a door open and two more shapes came out, one holding a lantern, walking away from the house, then back again in a little while.

We saw other shapes moving behind the windows.

"How many you figure?" Dew Hardy whispered.

"More than four by my count," I said.

"You think we ought to just wait for the posse?"

"It would just get confusing if we got into a firefight in the dark with that many folks running around . . . even if they were fighters, which I doubt they are. I'd just as soon it'd be you and me against those others. Leastways we know who is who."

"It'll be hell fighting in the dark like this, no matter if it's just us."

"It'll be to our benefit if we do it right."

"I don't know . . . it's a lot of men down there."

"It's not going to get any less if we wait."

"You want to just go in shooting?"

"You see them two smoking?" I said.

"Yeah, what about them."

"They're still outside, the others are inside."

"You want to take them first?"

"That's what I was thinking."

"Just eliminate them right off."

"Unless they want to surrender quiet."

"I doubt they will."

"Let's go find out."

Chapter Twenty-Six

Blackbird and Little Dick stood smoking outside the cabin, leery of being inside, sure a conspiracy of some sort might be taking place among that strange brood of white men. Blackbird's head was full of jangled considerations. It was Belle's plan that he kill Gypsy Davy and Little Dick, too, and that they'd take the money and head off toward San Francisco. But neither had counted on being introduced and staying among a bunch of bad fools like the Corns.

Blackbird was thinking he might have to kill everyone but Belle if they were to get away clean. It was a lot more killing than what he had planned on. The question was whether it was worth it. Something in him kept being tugged back to the Oklahoma pistol barrel, that Indian wife of his, and all those squalling kids. He didn't know what it was, or why, he just knew that it was.

It was Little Dick who suggested they sleep outside away from the house. Blackbird agreed.

Inside the house Gypsy had concluded his business with Belle and said in a panting manner: "It's time."

"For what?" she said.

"To tie up loose ends."

She was caught off guard by this sudden notion.

"What do you mean?"

"Kill Blackbird and Little Dick, then these Corns, if they raise a fuss."

She did her best to come up with a quick alternative plan and set it in motion. She'd already told Blackbird the plan to kill Davy and Little Dick, but hadn't counted on these lust-starved Corns. Now she and Blackbird would have to kill them all, a thought that she relished if she could figure out quickly how it was to be done—and how to alert Blackbird of Gypsy Davy's plot.

"Wait," she whispered, as Davy dressed and armed himself. "What if we wait until tomorrow when we're shut of this place?"

"Why put off tomorrow what can be done

tonight? Besides, those boys will never suspect it. And you know what the beauty of it all is? I'm going to have the Corns kill 'em, and then I'm going to kill the Corns. I told you I was a thinker."

She swallowed hard. Gypsy was no kind of lover compared to Blackbird and she figured in the long haul she could manipulate Blackbird a lot easier than she could the wily Gypsy.

"It's all set," he said, and turned himself out of the room.

Damn it all to hell! she thought, her mind a scramble as she shucked into her clothes.

Jack Corn had been doing some thinking of his own once the lovers had gone off to the only bedroom. The clan of them could hear Gypsy in the little room at work on Belle and it caused them to sweat in anticipation of doing the same thing with her as they listened.

"What we're going to do, children, is kill them fellers outside . . . that big nig and that little humped-back son-of-a-bitch," Jack Corn instructed his brood. "Then we'll do ol' Gypsy and keep whatever he surely has stole off somebody, and that woman, too. We won't ever have to go to town no more for beaver . . . not with a fine-looking woman like Belle. We'll keep her here for our own, and, when we ain't using her, she can cook and clean and other things for us, just like your old ma did before she went insane."

The plan delivered upon their ears brought the boys a certain bittersweet nostalgia about their late ma, but the prospect of having the beauty Belle at their disposal eradicated any such nostalgia for the old lady.

They looked at their pa eager as hunting hounds that had caught the scent of a fat rabbit.

"But we must take care, for Gypsy is a fast son-of-a-bitch with a gun, and them others is, too, by the looks of them," the old man intoned.

"We're plumb ready for whatever shakes out, Daddy," said Tobe.

"I think soon as things quiet down good and well, a couple of you boys sneak out and chop off the heads of that big buck and that little feller first. Then we come in and shoot old Davy so full of lead he'll leak blood for a month."

They nodded their heads as one.

"Tobe, you and Alonzo go quiet to the shed and get the axes."

Belle, as she was tugging on her britches, saw something pass by the window and paused in her dressing. Two shadows creeping toward the shape of a shed beyond the house. She could tell by the size of the shadows that neither shape was Blackbird or Little Dick and she knew full well how Gypsy walked bowlegged and it wasn't he, either.

Oh, God! Everything's started!

Fear crawled up her backbone like a centipede. A thrilling sort of fear like whenever blood was about to be shed. She just hoped she would be one of the ones shedding it. She never dreamed as a farm girl back in Iowa it could be like this.

Chapter Twenty-Seven

We slinked toward the house like a pair of stalking cats. Going slow so as not to make a sound, me carrying the 10-gauge and Dew Hardy his stolen pistol, both of us ready to do as much damage as necessary, but I was hoping not too much, because I was sick to death of killing and my heart just wasn't in it any more like it once was. I couldn't speak for Dew Hardy. He was a hard soul to figure. But I did not doubt he would do what he had to, for, in some ways, he seemed hard as slate on the inside.

Within a hundred yards of the cabin we saw the front door open, then close quickly, shutting out the light from inside. We saw a single man exit, and like me and the Pinkerton, stalking in his movements. Minutes earlier we'd watched the other two who'd been outside smoking go off together. We figured to bed down for the night.

"That's Gypsy Davy," Dew Hardy whispered.

"How can you tell?"

"By that big sombrero."

We caught the glint of a silver revolver in his hand by the moon's light. The moon was an orb of white like the light of freight train, only it wasn't moving.

"What's the son-of-a-bitch up to?" Dew mused.

"A man in the night with a gun in his hand," I said, "aims to kill them other two, I'm betting."

"Yeah . . . ," Dew started to say when suddenly the night erupted in a crackle of gunfire from the direction Davy had headed.

The gunfire was followed by screams, hoots and hollers, and loud curses. The muzzle flashes lit up the darkness like a swarm of fireflies—only real big fireflies and not the little kind. And then the gunfire came both within and without the cabin.

"What the god damn hell!" Dew Hardy exclaimed.

"I don't know but it sounds like they're killing each other," I said.

Dew Hardy turned to look at me, his face glowing like that of a ghost in the eerie light of the moon.

"You're shitting me, right?"

"Listen to it."

"I am."

"Keep listening."

"I am."

Bang! Bang! Bang! Bang! Bang! Bang!

There was the whiz and pop and ricochet of

flying lead and we both dropped to the ground for fear of stray bullets finding us. Our luck had been so bad lately it wouldn't have been inconceivable we'd be hit.

We laid there, watching as the gun flashes winked on and off with the bark of pistols in and around the cabin.

Strangely I felt a calm sense come over me.

"What'll we do?" Dew Hardy said.

"Nothing," I said. "Nothing at all."

"Yeah, that's sort of what I was thinking, too."

I took the makings from my pocket and rolled a shuck, then lit it, and laid there listening as murder took place.

Chapter Twenty-Eight

How it went down was this way.

Gypsy was about to shoot Blackbird who was lying on his side, knees pulled up, snoring softly. Nearby lay Little Dick, sleeping on his back, mouth open wide, snoring loudly.

Gypsy thumbed back the hammer of his pistol figuring to kill them quickly himself and not trust the Corns to get it done. Gypsy was a self-reliant type with mercurial musings. He'd decided at the last moment that he would himself kill the pair, then ambush the Corns, figuring

Blackbird and Little Dick were the more dangerous of the bunch.

But then, as he was about to pull the trigger, he saw two of the Corn boys enter a tool shed, and so wondered what they were doing, skulking around in the moonlight.

Davy had a bad feeling. He watched them emerge again, and they were carrying something but at first he could not tell what until at last the moon glinted off one of their axe blades.

Well, god damn. That old man is going to try and turn the tables, his wily instincts told him. *And why not? Wouldn't I do the same if I was that old bastard and a chance at that money? Oh, hell, and Belle, too. I seen the way they stared at her, drool coming out of their mouths. Those dirty sons-of-bitches.*

He cut loose on one and watched the figure drop like a stone as the other yelped like a scalded dog and ran for the house.

The shot awakened Blackbird and Little Dick who jumped up like a frog set on a hot skillet.

Blackbird saw Gypsy standing there with a pistol in his hand and figured rightly or wrongly that Davy had come to kill him. Blackbird drew his own piece from under his head, cocked and aimed it, but not before Davy turned again at the sound of a gun being cocked. Both men fired at once.

Davy's shot proved truer, and Blackbird fell

back dead before he could even give it a thought, his brains partly splattered across the face of Little Dick Longwinter.

Little Dick yelped and cussed and did a frenetic jig.

Inside the house Belle had come out the bedroom door and run smack into the old man and the three remaining Corn boys armed with gun, club, fry pan, and a knife respectively.

They saw her just as she saw them.

"Hey, little sister," Jack Corn said with his nearly toothless and lascivious grin. "The chickens are coming home to roost this night."

The boys cackled their delight.

The one they called Peckerwood said: "Dibs."

She shot him first, and he looked down at where the bullet had punched a hole in his middle, then puked all over himself before pitching over.

The other two came at her with knife and club.

"You stupid bastards," she said. "Don't you know nothing? Taking a knife and club to a gunfight!"

It was for her almost orgasmic to shoot them so quickly it sounded like she'd only fired once instead of twice. She saw a strawberry blossom just below the eye of the one boy and the other grabbed his throat. They both fell headlong, landing at her feet, the knife and club still gripped in their dirty hands.

Outside, she and the old man heard the gunfire.

"It's a bitch, ain't it?" the old man said as though taking delight in the mayhem. "I always knowed those children of mine would pass before me, and now they have. That leaves you and me." He aimed his rifle, a Sharp's Big Fifty, knowing and hating what damage it would do to her, but having no choice in the matter now.

"I was planning on diddling you whilst you was alive, but you leave me no choice . . . I'll just have to do it before you grow too cold and stiff. . . ."

He pulled the trigger, and she did, too.

Little Dick was scrambling around like a nervous debutante at her first ball, trying to avoid being shot dead by Gypsy Davy.

"What you doing?" he yelped at Davy, who himself had been shot and wounded by the off-mark bullet from Blackbird, blood dribbling from his rib meat.

Inches, Davy had thought when he felt the biting sting. *Difference between living and dying is just inches.*

"I come to kill you, Little Dick."

"For what? I didn't do nothing to you."

"You was going to steal my money."

"Steal your money? It was *our* money as I rightly recall. We all robbed that bank together."

"That was then, this is now."

Little Dick finally got his piece loose from its scabbard but in his haste shot himself in the foot and blew off the big toe of his right foot. He screamed and cussed and fell down and tried to get up again, not knowing whether to hold his foot or scramble for his dropped pistol.

"You might be a killer," Davy said, drawing a bead on the wounded man, "but you ain't a very good one."

He pulled the trigger, laying Little Dick out like a slab of butchered beef. Then Davy turned to the house to mop up whatever had gone on inside.

He found Belle sitting in the doorway of their love nest, holding back the blood with her hands that was leaking from her middle where the round had gone. It had come out through her spine and splintered the doorjamb. Across the room, the old man sat dead with his mouth agape and his legs stretched out in front of him like he'd gone to sit on a chair and someone had pulled it out from under him.

"I can't feel my legs," Belle said in great distress, looking up at Davy. "Help me stand."

Davy tried, but her legs flopped and wouldn't hold her. Then he felt in her back a warm wet ragged hole he could stick all his fingers in, and set her down gently as a vase full of freshly cut flowers.

"You're all ruined, Belle."

"No!" she screamed. It was the worst thing

Gypsy Davy ever heard a human say, the sound of her voice.

"That bullet took out some of your backbone."

She screamed again.

"God it hurts."

"I reckon so."

"Carry me out of this place," she pleaded.

He shook his head.

"Won't do you no good, Belle. I'm half shot myself. Think some of my ribs is broke."

"Where're the others? Where's Blackbird?"

"Stone cold dead."

Again Belle cried out, but Gypsy Davy knew it wasn't from pain this time.

"You and him were planning on running off, weren't you?" Davy said.

Belle shook her head.

"Don't lie to me now, Belle. It would be a sin to face Jesus with a lie on your lips."

Belle looked as forlorn as he'd ever seen a body look.

Her fingers tightened around his wrist as he tried to stand away from her.

"Don't leave me like this," she pleaded.

She was still beautiful of face but the rest of her was ruined, ruined, ruined, and they both knew it.

"Look yonder," Davy said, pointing toward the door.

And when she shifted her gaze in that direction, he shot her in the top of the head and quickly looked away because he did not want to see Belle Moon in further destruction.

His side burned like a fire inside his skin. He found the old man's whiskey jug and poured some over the wound, then took a swallow to fortify himself against whatever he must face. He figured to burn the place and light out after collecting the money he and Belle had stored under the bed. The sheets still smelled sweetly of her perfume as he pulled out the loot, and it caused a small lump in his throat to think he'd murdered the only body he thought he had ever loved.

But then he suddenly realized that one of the Corn boys was unaccounted for—the one outside earlier with the one he shot. The one who'd run off.

Where'd that little son-of-a-bitch get off to?

He decided wherever that other little rascal had fled, he was most likely a good mile from the house by now. Those boys did not have their old man's grit; you could see that in their weak eyes.

He stepped from the cabin.

Davy did not see the glint of axe blade arcing through the dark until it was too late.

The blade cut him clean through the neck, lopping off head with sombrero still attached by stampede string.

The head of Gypsy Davy with eyes open wide from surprise went rolling across the yard as the body folded like a deflated accordion.

Not so much as a word had Davy to say about his dying.

No time for eulogies or apologies or famous last words.

Many bandits died without giving speeches. Davy was simply one of the many.

The Corn boy stood breathless at his own brave act and was already beginning to fantasize about the reputation he would get from killing Gypsy Davy.

"Why it was easy as cutting the head off a chicken," he said to the night air, as though practicing a speech he'd give over and over again in saloons all the rest of his life. "That blade cut clean and true and Davy never stood a chance to pull them fast pistols of his."

Then two men stepped from the deeper shadows.

"Who you?" the boy demanded.

Chapter Twenty-Nine

When the shooting stopped, we rose up and walked to the house. It was still lit on the inside, but there were no more shadows passing back and forth.

We saw the kid swing the axe and Davy's sombrero-clad head go flying. He stood there, muttering to himself, blood wet on the axe's blade in the full moonlight.

It was about the bloodiest thing I ever saw. Dew Hardy raised his weapon to shoot the kid, but I pushed the pistol aside.

"Let it be," I said.

The kid looked at us, said: "Who you?"

I'd no doubt he would be willing to behead us, too, if we hadn't been armed, if he hadn't seen the 10-gauge in my hands.

"You better go on and get the hell out of here," I said.

"I'm already gone," the boy said, dropping the axe before running off into the night.

"Why didn't you just go ahead and shoot that little prick?" Dew Hardy said.

"There's been enough hell paid this night," I said. "He'll live or die the way he's meant to, but not by our hand, not this night."

Dew Hardy shook his head.

"You are one hard fellow to figure," he said.

"I guess that would make two of us," I said.

After we checked everything and saw that there was no one left alive, I felt drained of all emotion and rolled myself a shuck and smoked it. The night wind blew gently down from some distant unseen mountains and the moon shone over everything in a sad sort of way. It was almost too quiet, but then it always is quiet—following great violence.

Dew Hardy bent and picked up the moneybags still clutched in Davy's hands.

"Look what I found," he said.

"What do you intend to do with it?" I said.

"Finders keepers," he said.

"No," I said.

"You ain't intending on keeping it all for yourself," he said. "No god damn' way."

"I aim to take it back to the owners," I said. "The bank money and whatever is left from the stage robbery."

"All of it?"

"Yes, all of it."

"But ain't nobody going to know we got it if we ride off now."

"I'll know," I said.

"You ain't going to let me keep just a little . . . for our troubles?"

"Not a damned dime."

"What if I feel differently?"

"Then I guess this night has not seen the last of death," I said. I wasn't sure if I would shoot Dew Hardy if he put up a fight over the money, but I wasn't sure I wouldn't, either.

"I ain't afraid of you."

"Never thought you were."

"I could have just let you die back in that town."

"You could have."

"That don't count for nothing with you, that I saved your hide?"

"It does, but that's got nothing to do with stolen money."

"I've never seen nobody so ungrateful," he said.

"Then you've not met many," I said.

"Shit."

"You can still have whatever reward there is for Davy and them," I said. "Just sit tight until the law and that posse gets here and claim the reward for yourself."

"You don't want none of it, neither?"

"No."

"You think it's blood money?"

"I don't think nothing. I just don't want any."

"Well, I never met nobody like you in my life."

"See you around someday, maybe," I said.

We didn't shake hands, but I could feel his eyes on me as I walked away with the moneybags.

"So long, Messenger," I heard him say.

I didn't bother to look back.

About the Author

Bill Brooks is the author of twenty-one novels of historical and frontier fiction. After a lifetime of working a variety of jobs, from shoe salesman to shipyard worker, Brooks entered the health care profession where he was in management for sixteen years before turning to his first love—writing. Once he decided to turn his attention to becoming a published writer, Brooks worked several more odd jobs to sustain himself, including wildlife tour guide in Sedona, Arizona where he lived and became even more enamored with the West of his childhood heroes, Roy Rogers and Gene Autry. Brooks wrote a string of frontier fiction novels, beginning with *The Badmen* (1992) and *Buscadero* (1993), before he attempted something more lyrical and literary: *The Stone Garden: The Epic Life of Billy the Kid* (2002). This was followed in succession by *Pretty Boy: The Epic Life of Pretty Boy Floyd* (2003) and *Bonnie & Clyde: A Love Story* (2005). *The Stone Garden* was compared by *Booklist* with classics like *The Virginian* and *Hombre*. After that trio of novels, Brooks was asked to return to frontier fiction by an editor who had moved to a new publisher and he wrote in succession three series for them, beginning with

Law For Hire (2003), then, *Dakota Lawman* (2005), and finishing up with *The Journey of Jim Glass* (2007). He now lives in Indiana, in one of his several home towns. *The Messenger* is Brooks's twenty-second novel.

Center Point Large Print
600 Brooks Road / PO Box 1
Thorndike ME 04986-0001 USA

(207) 568-3717

US & Canada:
1 800 929-9108
www.centerpointlargeprint.com